THE FINAL CUT

JASPER BARK

Crystal Lake Publishing
www.CrystalLakePub.com

WELCOME
TO ANOTHER

CRYSTAL LAKE PUBLISHING
CREATION

Join today at www.crystallakepub.com & www.patreon.com/CLP

To Robert Bloch, Ramsey Campbell, Lisa Tuttle,
Robert Aickman. Clive Barker and Stephen King
for showing me what horror could be at a seminal
age.
I am forever in your debt.

GREETINGS, GENTLE READER AND WELCOME TO THE *BARK BITES HORROR LINE.* OUR FIRST OFFERING INVOLVES TWO ASPIRING FILMMAKERS WHO FIND THEMSELVES ABOUT TO STAR IN A SNUFF FILM.
A FATE MOST OF US WOULD RATHER AVOID, BUT IF FORTUNE FAVOURS OUR FILMMAKERS WITH A REPRISE THEY MAY YET REGRET IT.
FOR THE *FINAL CUT* IS ALWAYS THE DEEPEST, AS YOU'RE ABOUT TO FIND OUT, AS SOON AS YOU TURN THAT PAGE...
TUNÓN
BENZO

CHAPTER ONE

"S0, LET ME see if I've got this right," Ashkan paused for effect. Like a lot of gangsters, he fancied himself a bit of an actor. The Iranian Al Pacino was how he styled himself. Right now his well practised glare was boring a hole in Sam's forehead.

"You muppets borrowed fifty grand of my money, my fucking money, to shoot a feature film. Ten days you said, ten days to shoot it. Two months to edit it, then blam, stick it out on the net as video on demand and we'll recoup the cost in a matter of weeks. Am I lying?"

"No," said Sam, appalled at how high and frightened his voice sounded. "Look if you just give us a bit of time we can . . . "

Ashkan brought the back of his hand across Sam's face. The blow sent Sam sprawling and the only reason he didn't fall out of the chair was because he was held there with duct tape. The side of his face stung and it took a second for his vision to come back into focus.

"When it's your cue to fucking speak I'll tell you, alright?" said Ashkan. Sam nodded and his head throbbed. Ashkan drew himself up to his full height. At six five he was pretty imposing. He adjusted his leather jacket and smoothed down his Ben Sherman shirt like he was about to go on stage. Then he looked from Sam to Jimmy, who was duct taped to the chair next to him.

"See, what really disappoints me is, I like you guys. I like what you do. You're good at it. So I put in a little sweetener. I let you off the interest for six whole months. That should've been enough time to clear the whole debt. Now, some people might think I was going soft. But I saw it as an investment in my acting career. You guys were writing me a big part in the movie, so it was the least I could do. So yesterday, I rock up at the set with my crew, looking to show off me mad acting skills and what do I find, Farshad?"

"These two cunts, with their dicks in their hands and fuck all else," said Farshad, a short guy with a thick beard and huge shoulders. He was standing behind Sam and Jimmy.

"That's right," said Ashkan. "And trust me guys, as far as dicks go, they weren't that impressive. I was expecting lights, cameras, the whole fucking shebang. Instead I got mugged off. No equipment, no script, no fucking actors, just you two cunts in an empty fucking warehouse. That's all I got to show for my fifty grand. Am I lying?"

Sam and Jimmy shook their heads.

"You know what else I found out? Last week you two pissants tried to buy fifty grand's worth of coke from one of my rivals. One of my fucking rivals! Only someone pulled a gun as it was going down and you were left with fuck all to show for yourselves. What were you gonna do with all that coke? Sell it to your friends in the film biz?"

Sam and Jimmy looked at each other, then nodded hesitantly.

"So you never had any intention of making a film then?"

Sam didn't know what to do.

"You can talk now," said Ashkan.

"No, we're still going to make the film," said Sam. "I swear we're going to make it, but we had overheads. I maxed out all my cards funding our last feature and costs were spiralling. We were going to take the profits from the coke and plough it all back into the film, I swear to you we were."

"Whose idea was this?"

"It . . . it was mine," Jimmy croaked, after a long pause. He was sweating heavily, it ran in trickles from his chestnut curls and pooled in his beard. He blinked nervously.

"Jimmy thought we could use some of his underworld contacts and bring the deal off quickly," said Sam.

"Oh yeah," said Ashkan with a derisive snort. "Big man is Jimmy, really well connected. See, what I don't understand is, I just found you got some huge fucking trust fund waiting for you. So what the fuck you getting mixed up with all this shit for?"

Sam hung his head. "It's my parents," he said in a small voice.

"What?"

"It's my fucking parents. They won't let me access the fund until I get a proper job, in the City or something, raping third world countries."

"You have to admit they've got a point. I mean you wouldn't be in this mess if you had a proper job and I wouldn't be about to do this."

Ashkan clicked his fingers. Faisal, one of the thugs

who'd grabbed Sam and Jimmy and driven them to the Bethnal Green lock up, sidled up to Ashkan. He was tall and rangy, with a thick black moustache and a scar down his left cheek. He handed Ashkan a syringe. It was the big, thick kind you find in hospitals, not the sort you get at a needle exchange. It was full of clear liquid.

Ashkan grabbed hold of Jimmy's hair and bent his head to one side. A blue vein throbbed on Jimmy's neck, Ashkan plunged the syringe into it.

"Jesus, Ashkan," Jimmy screamed, "What the fuck, what the fuck?"

"Just giving you a little taste innit," said Ashkan, pushing the plunger. "Thought you boys liked this sorta shit."

"The fuck is it?" Jimmy looked like he was going to have a fit. The muscles in his legs spasmed and his eyes twitched.

"This shit? This is better than meth, better than any of that crap you get on the street. This is from my private collection. Save it for special occasions, like this one." Ashkan clicked his fingers and one of his flunkies handed him another syringe.

"Please," said Sam, as Ashkan approached. "Not the neck, please."

"It's better in the jugular vein, innit. Goes straight to the brain see. Gives you twice the fucking hit—Blam!"

Sam felt a sharp prick as the needle hit his vein and the drug shot into his blood. His heart hammered like he was going into cardiac arrest and an ice cold wave washed over him. All the hairs on his body stood on end. The mother of all rushes charged through him. Ashkan hadn't lied, this stuff was powerful. Sam's head began to shake and his jaw worked involuntarily. He was blinking about a hundred times a minute.

Faisal put a laptop down on a card table in front of them. "Have I got your attention? Good. Wouldn't want you to miss a minute of this." Ashkan opened the laptop. "You boys like film shows don't you? Well I've got one mother of a film for you." He clicked an icon on the screen and a piece of footage came up. "See this? This is what happens when you fuck with me. When you take my money and mug me off in front of my crew." Ashkan patted Sam and Jimmy on the shoulders. "Enjoy the show boys."

The footage showed a dimly lit stone room that could have been a cellar or a prison cell. The camera, held by an amateur, swung unsteadily about the space. It picked out three figures, two men and a woman, strapped to operating tables which were covered in thick plastic sheeting.

One of the men was screaming and sobbing, snot streamed down his top lip as he writhed and fought his straps. The other man, from his expression, was bargaining for his life. He looked Mediterranean, but was shouting in a language that sounded Arabic.

The woman couldn't have been a bigger contrast. She lay very still, her body completely relaxed and her face serene. She seemed completely at peace with what was going to be done to her.

She was very striking, with strawberry blonde hair and high cheekbones. Her curves suggested a sensuous nature, but her eyes seemed to look heavenward, giving her a saintly, almost beatific look.

"This the tape you got from Mr Isimud?" said Farshad.

"Yeah man," replied Ashkan. "This is some seriously fucked up shit, seriously fucked up."

"Sweet, wanted to see this for ages."

"Some of the things they do man, they're like artists, trust me, artists—not killers." Ashkan smacked Sam and Jimmy on the back of the head. He reached over their shoulders and pointed at the screen. "Pay attention boys, this is my money back guarantee. I guarantee this will happen to you if I don't get my money back."

CHAPTER TWO

THE CAMERA PUSHED in to a close shot of the Mediterranean guy's face. He was still babbling desperately as two dark figures moved in on either side. The figures were blurry shadows, underlit and out of focus. Sam wasn't sure how they'd achieved the effect because the Mediterranean guy's face was crystal clear, so were the scalpels the figures held.

The blurry figures moved in unison, as though choreographed. They stretched a tight strap across the guy's forehead to keep his head still. Only his eyes rolled wildly as he pleaded for his life. Then the figures each took hold of an eyelid and pried them apart.

With their other hands the figures brought the scalpels down into the corners of the guy's eyes. Using tiny, deft movements they severed the muscle tissue holding his eyeballs in place. The guy stopped imploring the figures and shrieked with pain and fear.

Thin streams of blood spurted from the guy's eye sockets. The figures put down their scalpels and each produced a set of forceps. They took hold of his eyeballs with the forceps and lifted them out of their sockets, pulling them as far as their optic nerves would stretch. Next they turned the eyeballs so the pupils were pointed at the guy's mouth. Working together, as though their free hands belonged to the same body, the figures applied dental clamps to the guy's mouth and forced his jaws apart, holding his eyeballs over his mouth the whole while.

With the clamps in place, the figures picked up their scalpels again and took to slicing off the guy's top and bottom lips. Blood sprayed the cornea of one eyeball and Sam realised that, as the optic nerves were still attached, the guy could still see out of his severed eyes. He was being forced to watch an extreme close up of his own mutilation.

When the lips were removed, the hand of one figure produced a tiny chisel and held it over the guy's front tooth. It was the sort of delicate tool a sculptor would use to apply the finishing touches to a marble bust. The other figure's hand brought a mallet into shot.

The camera pushed in to a close up of the guy's open mouth and throat. The mallet struck the chisel on his front tooth, with such swift force, that the tooth was not only knocked out of its gum, it embedded itself in the lining of the guy's throat.

The guy choked and yelled in agony, his throat going into spasms. The figures continued to knock his teeth out, angling the chisel with such precision, and striking it with such power, that each of the teeth was driven into a different part of the guy's throat. When they were done the whole of his gullet was raw and torn and lined with teeth.

"Jesus this is fucking hardcore," said Farshad. "Is this for real?"

"Dunno," said Ashkan. "Ain't seen this bit before."

"Thought you said you'd watched it all the way through? Twice now."

"I have, I just ain't seen this bit before. Must be some glitch or something."

The camera pulled back from the ruined face of the Mediterranean guy. The figures left him and moved on to the woman. Two more figures joined them at her side. Sam started to cry and tried not to watch as they went to work on her. Jimmy started to hyperventilate next to him.

What they were doing to the woman was a hundred times worse than the damage they'd inflicted on the Mediterranean guy. She didn't scream or fight them, and that made watching even worse. She just opened her mouth and let out a silent cry of anguish so profound it transcended the desecration of her flesh.

"Aww man, that ain't right!" said someone behind them, his voice loud with disgust. "That ain't right."

Every time Sam or Jimmy tried to close their eyes or turn away Ashkan punched them both in the back of the head. "Ashkan, please man," said Sam. "You don't need to show us anymore. You've made your point; you'll get your money. Honestly, even if I have to sell everything, you'll get your money. Just don't make me watch any more. Please don't make me watch anymore."

The drug in Sam's system made him even more susceptible to the footage. He could feel everything they were doing to the woman. Ashkan ignored his pleas; he was mesmerised and appalled by what was happening on the laptop.

There were groans and cries of disgust from the other men in the room. "Turn it off man," said one. "Turn it off, we've seen enough." Another man started wailing and broke into a sob.

"Can't turn it off," said Ashkan. "They've got to watch this to the end. They have to learn."

But the men in the room had all had enough. Jimmy heard two of them turn to leave the lock up. "Alright," said Ashkan. "We'll leave them to watch the end of it and we'll go for a smoke."

Ashkan and his men were standing behind Sam and Jimmy. It was more intimidating that way. It also made it hard for Sam to work out what was happening. He glanced away from the screen to look at Jimmy. Jimmy had his eyes tightly shut. He'd had enough, but Ashkan was too distracted to notice.

Sam closed his eyes, too. He didn't want to watch any more footage; it was becoming unbearable. The drugs had left his nerve endings raw.

Someone's footsteps approached them. Sam winced automatically, expecting a blow, but the footsteps went straight past him. He heard tapping on the laptop keyboard. Were they trying to switch it off?

"Fuck," a voice said in front of him. Sam didn't recognise it. "Fuck NO! FUCK!"

The sound of something very sharp going into flesh followed. Then a sudden release of breath, as if the air had been knocked out of someone. Cries of alarm and disbelief rang out behind Sam, then broke off, becoming throttled chokes and coughs.

Sam pulled his chin into his chest and hunched his shoulders. Trying to make himself as small as he could while still taped to a chair. He could feel tears welling up behind eyelids that were screwed shut.

The whole lock-up was filled with the wet ripping of torn flesh and the crackling snap of fractured bones. It was like someone had recorded a slaughterhouse and then played it at triple speed. Only the sounds weren't coming from the tinny laptop speaker, they were all around him.

Sam couldn't look, couldn't open his eyes. He just froze. Every sound made him shake more. What were Ashkan and the others doing to Jimmy? Why didn't he scream? How could the noise be so deafening?

Sam was next, he knew that. He gritted his teeth but it didn't hold back the sobs that were breaking from his chest. The front of his jeans became warm and wet as his bladder emptied.

One single thought went round and round in his mind.

Please let it be quick.

Please let it be quick.

Please let it be quick.

CHAPTER THREE

A **HOT JET** of liquid hit Sam in the back of the head. He gasped and started to hyperventilate.

"No, please . . . don't," he said in a high pitched voice. He hated the way he sounded, but he still begged. "Please, please don't. Oh God don't."

Nothing happened.

He ground his teeth and waited for the first blow.

It didn't come.

This was worse than torture.

"Just do it, okay. Just fucking do it!"

"Sam?" it was Jimmy's voice.

Sam opened his eyes and stole a glance at Jimmy. The back of Jimmy's head was dripping with viscera.

The lock up was dead quiet. Something was wrong. There were thick gobs of blood and torn flesh on Sam's shoulders. He could feel it dripping from his man bun down the back of his neck.

"Jimmy," Sam said. "Are you okay?"

"I think so, how about you?"

"I dunno, are you sure you're okay? The back of your head is covered in blood."

"Yeah, but I'm pretty sure none of its mine. You?"

"They never touched me. I kept waiting for them to do something, but they never did."

"What happened to Ashkan and the others? Why are we covered in blood?"

"I don't know."

Sam rocked back and forth to turn his chair round and get a better look at the lock up. The floor was slick with blood and his feet skidded. It smelled of fear and blood, like an abattoir.

The whole lock up had changed colour. It was now a deep crimson. All the walls and surfaces were covered in blood. It was raining down in fat drops from the ceiling. Much of it had congealed into the thick puddles filled with heaps of pulverised flesh and bone.

What the hell had Ashkan and his men done? Where the hell had they gone? He looked about the room and saw tiny scraps of clothing that he recognised, in amongst the gore. Then it slowly hit Sam. He was looking at them. This was all that remained of his tormentors.

This was humanity broken down into its essential components. This was what lay beneath the skin of everyone. This is what happened when you tore out the insides of a person and ground them into little pieces. Raw, fragile and utterly ruined.

None of his captors' violence or selfishness justified this. This was something no human being should ever have to suffer. Sam felt his stomach lurch. He bent his head and emptied his guts onto the blood soaked floor.

"You okay?" said Jimmy.

"Yeah," said Sam. "Must've been a bad pint."

Jimmy laughed at this. A short high pitched giggle that was more hysterical than anything.

"The hell just happened man?"

"I have no idea, had my eyes closed the whole time."

"Me, too."

"This is sick man, this is un-fucking-believable. This is worse than anything we saw on that footage. They've been butchered, all of them."

"Is that even them? I mean, shit, that doesn't look like any human remains I've ever seen. I've seen enough photos by now, so have you. They look like ground pork, like someone's put them through a meat grinder."

"How is that even possible? This sort of damage should take hours. I wasn't timing it or anything, but I swear we only had our eyes closed for five or six minutes."

"I dunno, maybe it's the drugs."

"You think?"

"Ever been this high on meth or coke before?"

"Shit no. How could I? I hardly do that stuff."

"Well I do, and this is hardcore. Who knows how much it's fucking with our brains. We might have been in here for days for all we know."

"No I don't think so." Sam shook his head and sprayed blood on his chinos.

A long, thin strip of human skin peeled off the ceiling above them and landed with wet slap on the floor.

"So who do you think did this?" said Jimmy. "I mean they didn't do this to each other, that's insane."

"I haven't a clue. It's beyond me. I can't imagine what sort of person is capable of this."

"Why didn't they kill us? How come we were spared?"

"Maybe they didn't see us."

"How could they miss us? We're right in the middle of the place."

"We probably don't matter to whoever did this. Maybe it's some gangland thing, a reprisal or whatever. They saw us taped up and realised we weren't a threat. Plus we had our eyes closed so we can't identify anyone."

"What if they come back to finish us off? Tie up loose ends and stuff?"

"Haven't they cleared off before the cops get here?"

"Are the cops coming?"

"They must be."

"Who'd call them? It's totally remote here, no-one would have heard a thing."

"We're in the middle of a city. Someone must have heard."

"I'm not sure I want the cops here."

"Why? They can't pin any of this on us. We're the victims here."

"We're the only ones left alive, I don't think they'll see us as victims. Besides, what if it comes out that we were gonna offload a serious amount of blow? We could do a lot of time for that."

"We didn't actually sell any drugs though."

"No but I told a lot of people we were going to."

"Why the fuck would you do that?"

"I was trying to build up a client base. It's called basic marketing."

Sam sighed as another rush went through him, making his skin tingle. "It doesn't matter now. We need to get out of here before anyone else comes."

"Easy for you to say, I'm kinda taped to a chair, remember?"

"Think I can fix that," said Sam.

The duct tape went around his chest and arms and both his ankles, holding him to the chair. His cardigan was quite baggy and Sam was pretty sure he could get his left arm out. He was taller and skinnier than Jimmy, so he that gave him more room to manoeuvre. Ashkan had only wanted to scare them, so Faisal hadn't been too worried about Sam and Jimmy escaping when he taped them up.

This said, Sam nearly dislocated his shoulder getting his left arm free. He leaned a bit too far to the right getting it out of the sleeve and his chair toppled over. He expected to get a face full of blood as he cracked his cheek on the floor, but there didn't seem as much of it as he thought. When the shooting pains in the side of his head had subsided, he saw there was only a thin smear of blood on the ground. He'd thought there was more. Maybe it had soaked into the concrete.

With a little more wriggling Sam got his right arm free and was able to set the chair back up on its legs. Then he went to work on the tape round his ankles.

"You okay?" said Jimmy.

"Got a sore face and shoulder," said Sam, as he found the corner of the tape and began peeling it of his right ankle. "But I'll live." His left ankle was more difficult, he couldn't get it loose.

"Sam look," said Jimmy, nodding his head towards a load of crates nearby. In front of them, in a pool of blood on the ground, was a Stanley knife. It must have fallen out of one of the men's pockets.

With his left leg still stuck to the chair, Sam stood unsteadily up and moved over to the crates, dragging the chair along with him. He picked up the knife and chopped through the tape round his ankle.

"Thanks," Jimmy said, as Sam sliced the tape holding him to the chair. Jimmy was shorter than Sam by a good two or three inches, but he was broader across the shoulders and had a stockier frame. This made it harder to get him loose. Jimmy's winced as Sam sliced through the tape and into the back of his jacket, nicking his skin as he went.

"Ow, watch it," Jimmy cried,

"Sorry, think I ruined your jacket too."

"Just get me out."

Sam cut the rest of the tape and Jimmy got to his feet, stretching his arms and shoulders and stamping his feet to get the life back into them. Sam expected him to send up splashes of blood, but it seemed there was less of it on the floor than ever. It had stopped dripping from the ceiling too. Sam looked up and saw only a thin film, where previously it had been soaked.

The piles of diced flesh and bone looked smaller too, as though they'd shrunk inexplicably. Sam shook his head. The drugs had obviously affected him more than he realised. He dropped the knife and headed towards the large metal doors that led out of the lock up.

"Wait," Jimmy called out after him. Sam turned. Jimmy was pointing at the laptop. "What about this?"

"What about it?"

"We can't just leave it here."

"Of course we can."

"It's a potential goldmine."

"A what?"

"A goldmine. Have you ever seen anything sicker than this footage?"

"Err, take a look around you."

"I mean on film?"

"I couldn't watch most of it."

"Exactly, and we shoot this kind of thing for a living."

"But the stuff we shoot is all make up and effects."

"And sometimes people can see that. You've read the write ups."

"So we're not Tom Savini, so what."

"We could be, with this. No-one's seen anything like it. This is more extreme than American Guinea Pig or anything."

"No," Sam was incredulous. "No fucking way! Are you out of your fucking mind?"

"No, hear me out. There are a lot of sick fucks out there that would pay through the nose to see this."

"No-one could sit through the whole footage. We couldn't take it and neither could Ashkan or his cronies and those guys are killers."

"So we don't use the whole footage. We cut it up into little clips, just enough to really freak people out, and we build a whole story around them."

"I can't believe you're suggesting this."

"Think about it from an economic point of view. After the kit, make up and effects are our biggest expense. We don't need much kit to shoot a story around this footage and we won't need any make up or effects. It'll take our budget down to nothing."

"Well nothing is all we have at the moment."

"At least we no longer owe fifty grand to a bloodthirsty loan shark."

"Well, there is that."

Sam looked at the flesh heaps, trying to work out

which one had been Ashkan. He could have sworn they'd gotten smaller still. His resistance to Jimmy's idea was also shrinking. In a strange way, Jimmy was making a warped kind of sense.

"Would it work though?" Sam said.

"We could make it work. Please Sam, I need this."

"You need this?"

"I need something good to come out of this. Shit, look at us, look at this place. It's covered in blood, we're covered in blood." Maybe the blood had congealed, but Sam noticed Jimmy didn't seem quite so covered anymore. Jimmy continued: "This is worse than getting jacked by that coke dealer. This is worse than anything." Jimmy's mouth started to twitch and he let out a sob.

"Keep it together man," Sam said.

Jimmy picked up the laptop and held it to his chest, like a comfort blanket. "I need to make something positive come out of this. Otherwise what's the point of living through it?"

"Does there have to be a point?"

"Yes there does.!"

"But we survived, that's all there is to it, isn't that enough?"

"We won't survive though. I won't survive, not emotionally, not mentally. You know my history man, you know what happened with Jennie. I need something to get me through this."

Jimmy was starting to get loud and shrill. Sam held his hands up to quiet him. "Okay, okay, take it then."

Sam glanced round the lock up one last time. His eye fell on a bunch of cardboard boxes piled up against the wall. He went to check them out. The lock up was full of dodgy goods, some of them stolen, some seized in lieu of debt.

He wasn't sure why he ignored the voice at the back of his mind screaming for him to leave, but he began to rummage in the boxes. He thought about Ashkan and the things he threatened and Sam felt a wave of anger. Fuck that prick, he owed them this.

"What you doing?" said Jimmy joining him.

"Look at this," Sam pulled a Sony XDCAM from the bottom of the box. The mic cover was missing, but apart from that it was fine.

"PMW-300, professional quality, nice."

Sam and Jimmy exchanged a look. Geeking out over cameras felt almost normal. Maybe they could salvage something from this after all.

"Come on," said Sam. "Let's get out of here."

As they headed for the exit Sam tried to ignore the fact that half the blood had disappeared from the ceiling and the floors.

CHAPTER FOUR

IT WAS A short walk to Bethnal Green Road but it seemed to take forever to Sam. The sun was really bright and he felt ridiculously exposed. He was dripping with blood and he'd wet himself, how could he not attract attention.

Sam and Jimmy kept to the back streets. The blood dried quickly and seemed almost to evaporate, disappearing as mysteriously as the blood in the lock up. No-one paid them any attention when they hit the main road. Typical Londoners, ignoring everything they didn't want to see.

Sam tried hailing a couple of black cabs but they weren't having any of it. Eventually an empty one pulled up at some traffic lights and they tried to jump in.

"Sorry lads," said the driver, a middle aged guy with thinning hair and brown teeth. "But I can't have you in the back like that."

"Please," said Sam. "We've got to get out of here. It's all dried, we won't ruin your upholstery."

"Listen, whatever it is, I'm not interested. I don't want any trouble."

"It's not like you think," said Jimmy. He pointed to the camera Sam was holding. "We've shooting a . . . err, zombie film, that's all. This is just make up."

The driver shook his head. "Sorry lads, not gonna happen." He pulled away as the light turned green.

"You boys need a cab?" said a voice behind them. They turned and saw a Turkish guy standing by a car in a little side street.

"Are you a taxi?" said Jimmy.

"Mini-cab," the guy said and pointed to an office half way down the side street. The sign outside said: 'Yilmaz Cars.' "Just about to knock off for the day. Where you going?"

"Camden," Jimmy said, and gave him Sam's address.

"Hop in," said the guy opening the back door.

Sam climbed into the back seat and let Jimmy ride shotgun. He didn't feel like talking to the driver. His heart lurched and he started to shiver involuntarily. The drug in his system was wearing off. It was incredibly potent, but obviously didn't last very long. And the come down was a killer.

"Lived here long?" said the driver as he turned off Old Street onto City Road.

"Not in Camden," said Jimmy. "That's where my friend lives. But I've lived in various parts of London all my life. How about you?"

"London born and bred, same as yourself. City's changed a lot since I was a child in the 70s though."

"I'll bet it has. It's changed a lot since I was a kid. Not just the odd building either, whole streets and stuff. You wouldn't recognise it in some places."

"Cities are constantly changing," said the driver, turning to Jimmy. Even from the back seat Sam could see a thoughtful look cross his face. "That's part of their nature. But it's also part of their nature to hold their original purpose. They're a bit like ancient stories. Every generation tells them in a different way, adds new passages, leaves out old ones, but the essential idea remains the same. You might dress it up, so that a contemporary audience finds it more relevant to them, but the core concept is timeless. That's what gives them power, that's why people keep telling them."

"And you think cities are the same?"

"Definitely. We might tear down old streets and throw up new buildings for modern needs, but the reasons people come to the city, and gather in certain locations, never changes."

"Even when all the old places are gone?"

"The old places are never really gone. They're still there, right under the surface of the city."

"You mean underground."

"No, just hidden, often in plain view. You just need to know where to look for them, what turnings to take. They're still there, whenever you need to find them. Like really old stories that lie beneath the surface of the new ones. Giving them shape and form, drawing people back to them over the centuries."

"Wow, you're quite a philosopher aren't you?"

The driver smiled and shook his head. "No, I spend a lot of time driving round with just myself for company. Gives you the space to do a lot of thinking, you know what I mean?"

"Yeah, I hear you," said Jimmy.

Sam knew Jimmy was talking to the driver to take his mind off coming down. He was fidgeting and shuddering as the drug wore off. The driver chose not to see this. He'd probably ferried all kinds of people around in his car. Sam doubted anything would surprise him, not from the way he was talking.

The driver motioned to the back seat with his thumb. "So how about your friend, he from London too?"

"No, he's from Surrey, what you might call an off-comer, or an adopted son."

The driver nodded. Sam was mildly irritated by how much personal info Jimmy was giving away. What if the police questioned the driver later about the two blood stained guys he picked up?

Sam stared out of the window as they approached the Angel tube station. Two lanes of the road were cordoned off and several police directed the slow moving traffic into the remaining lane. As they pulled into the far lane, Sam glimpsed a Ford Mazda by the side of the road. It's windscreen was shattered and its front bonnet crumpled. The numbness Sam felt, about the slaughter he'd just seen, melted at the sight of blood on a lamppost. His mood was plummeting with the comedown and it all became too real for him. His vision blurred as tears filled his eyes.

The driver put his left hand over a tiny ivory statue on top of his dashboard. It was two faced, like the Roman god Janus, but this statue had an old crone on one side and a beautiful maiden on the other. The driver muttered something that might have been a prayer, in a language Sam didn't recognise. Then he placed two fingers on his forehead, right in the middle of his eyebrows, and touched a small gold pendant hanging from his rearview mirror. It was a mystical symbol, but not one Sam recognised.

Sam hadn't noticed either the statue or the

pendant when they got into the mini-cab. It was as though the driver had conjured them into being as soon as he touched them. Sam shook his head. That sounded crazy. It was the comedown affecting his mind.

The driver shot them a sheepish smile. "Just a prayer," he said. "For any spirits that might be abroad, newly separated from their bodies."

"Is that like, a Muslim thing?" said Jimmy gesturing towards the pendant and statue.

The driver's smile became broader and more knowing. "No, these are artefacts from far older beliefs."

"Like from Atlantis and shit?"

"Atlantis is a myth, these beliefs are much older than any myth."

"Doesn't all myth start with some basis of truth?" Jimmy was really getting into this debate. It was probably the best thing he could do, under the circumstances, but it made Sam uncomfortable. Talk of 'spirits separated from their bodies' reminded him of Ashkan and the ruined remains of the other men.

"All myth starts as story," said the driver. "Sometimes we call the story history, sometimes religion, eventually it all becomes myth. Beneath every myth is an ancient tale, a hidden belief that gives shape and form to every god that's ever received a prayer on a dark and lonely night."

"Okay, now you're getting wa-ay deep. Does this 'ancient belief' have a name then?"

"It's had many names, in every language ever spoken. Some call it 'the Oldest Truth,' others—the 'Faith that Came before Man.'"

"What do you call it?"

"I don't have to name my faith, I just have to live by it."

Maybe turning into Sam's street emboldened him, but it was at that point he decided to join the conversation.

"By praying for the spirits of car crash victims," he said, with a touch of derision in his voice. "Is that how you live by this ancient faith?"

"Yes," said the driver. "And by other acts of charity. Like picking up two young men covered in blood and carrying stolen goods, when no-one else would dream of giving them a lift."

The driver pulled up to the kerb. Jimmy hung his head. Sam went cold all over and paid without saying another word.

"He knows," said Jimmy. It was a warm evening, but he shivered as the mini-cab pulled away.

"He doesn't know anything," said Sam and hustled Jimmy indoors.

CHAPTER FIVE

SAM CLOSED HIS apartment door then slumped against it. Jimmy, already in the hallway, turned and caught his eye.

No words were necessary. More passed between them in that look than either could have spoken aloud. Sam felt a cold shudder move through him as he came down from the drug . It was wearing off and so was the adrenalin that had kept him going till now.

"I'm going to go grab a shower," Sam said, trying to keep his voice from breaking into a sob. He had to hold it together in front of Jimmy, had to be strong for him. He knew how much Jimmy needed that right now.

The scalding hot water couldn't stop Sam from shivering as he stood beneath it and wept. Images of the footage raced through his mind, mingling with the sounds of Ashkan and his men being butchered. He wanted the water to penetrate his skull and wash them all from his brain. With each powerful sob that escaped him, he admitted the weight they exerted on his soul and how indelibly they'd marked him. He would never be rid of them.

He pulled the tie from his man bun and lathered his hair with shampoo, working it into the thick clumps of dried blood that clung to the back of his head. It dripped down his shoulders and over his arms, but it seemed to disappear before it reached shower floor. Sam told himself it was the chemicals in his shampoo, but he didn't really believe that.

After changing into clean clothes, Sam walked from his bedroom to the living room where he found Jimmy, perched on the sofa, with his head in his hands, staring at the closed laptop on the coffee table. Jimmy's eyes were red and his cheeks were wet with tears but he wasn't making a sound.

Sam placed a hand on Jimmy's shoulder. "Come on," he said. "You need a shower too." He helped Jimmy to stand and he guided him to the bathroom. Jimmy was sinking into himself. Sam had known him long enough to know this wasn't a good thing. He needed to break the spiral, or Jimmy would go under and sink into a deep depression. Sam always took control when it came to practical matters. It was his role in their relationship and, at the moment, concentrating on someone else's troubles, helped take his mind off his own.

Sam told him to leave his clothes outside the bathroom door and collected them while Jimmy washed. Sam carried the soiled clothes out to the balcony and dumped them in the barbecue he kept out there. Already the blood stains looked old and were beginning to fade. Sam dowsed both their clothes in lighter gel and set a match to them.

As the flames consumed the clothing, Sam gazed down at Regents Canal beneath his balcony. Houseboats drifted lazily and couples walked hand in hand along the tow path, smug and content because they could afford the house prices in this part of town.

"The fuck you doing?" said Jimmy, standing at the french doors with a towel round his waist.

"What does it look like?"

"It looks like you're burning my three hundred quid jeans!"

"What else was I supposed to do?" Sam glanced over the balcony to make certain he wasn't in earshot of anyone, then lowered his voice. "They're covered in blood." Jimmy stared at him with mounting fury, not saying anything. "Blood that could link us to the lock up. If the police find a way to tie us to that we're fucked."

"Three hundred quid they cost me."

"You can buy more jeans."

"I don't own anything that cost more than those jeans."

"Well what were you doing spending three hundred quid on a pair of jeans?"

"You're a fine one to fucking talk."

"Okay, you can take a pair of my jeans, or whatever else you want. You're going to have to borrow something of mine to get home anyway."

"How am I going to fit into a pair of your jeans, you tall, skinny fuck?"

"Fine I'll buy you a new pair of jeans, happy now? A three hundred quid pair of jeans that aren't covered in blood."

"They were a limited edition. Besides that's not the point, I could have washed them."

"No you couldn't, they've got tests and stuff. Forensic science that can find traces in the fibres and shit, even after they're washed."

"It probably wouldn't even be there tomorrow. I mean it was already . . . "

"What?"

Jimmy shook his head. Neither of them was prepared to talk about the way the blood was slowly disappearing. It was one thing too many to dwell on, or even admit.

"We're going to have to get rid of that laptop too."

"What?!" Jimmy's furrowed his brow, fury building to outrage. "No way, no fucking way!"

"We have to, it's the only other thing that connects us to the lock up. If the police find it we're fucked, game over."

"Why would the police find it?"

"Cos they could get a warrant and search both our places."

"But why would they get a warrant? We didn't commit those murders."

"No but our DNA is all over that lock up, clothes fibres, hair, all sorts of stuff."

"So what? You've just burned the clothes and our DNA isn't on file anywhere, why would they link any of this to us? No one saw us leave or enter the place. There's nothing that puts us in the frame."

"There's that laptop, with footage of three other murders on it. What if they find that and think we're Henry Lee Lucas, massacring people and making snuff movies?"

"They won't find it. They're not going to investigate us!" Jimmy's tone was becoming more and more shrill.

"But what if they do, we can't take the chance."

Jimmy looked for a second like he was going to reply, but chose instead to pick an earthenware table lamp off the bookshelf and throw it out the french doors with an angry scream. The lamp shattered as it hit the barbecue and knocked it over, scattering the contents. Before Sam could gather up and put out the flaming clothes, Jimmy began to sweep DVDs, Blu-Rays and books from the shelves, many of them signed collectors' items.

Sam had only seen him like this once before, after the whole business with Jennie. He'd been angry with himself then, full of self-recrimination and he'd trashed his student digs. This was different. He'd been kidnapped, drugged, mentally tortured and was a witness to an atrocity neither of them could explain. He'd been pushed too far. They both had.

Sam made no effort to stop Jimmy. In a way he was relieved to see Jimmy snap. It meant he didn't have to. It was as if Jimmy was having an angry breakdown for both of them. It meant Sam didn't have to deal with what he was feeling. He could let Jimmy vent and pick up the pieces afterwards, like he always did.

Jimmy kicked over the sofa, then sank to his knees and started to cry again, but not silently this time. The laptop sat, like a brooding presence on the coffee table, miraculously unharmed. Sam knelt down next to his friend and put an arm around his shoulders.

"Okay," he said. "We'll keep the laptop, we'll make the movie."

"I need this."

"I know."

"We both do."

Sam held his friend as the anger drained from him.

"This is gonna sound really strange," Jimmy said

after a pause. "But I feel like we're supposed to do this. Like we don't have a choice. Like it was waiting for us."

"The laptop?"

"No the footage on it. It's like a story that's waiting to be told, waiting for us to tell it."

CHAPTER SIX

"SO WHO'S SENDING him these links?" said Sam.

"What?"

"Who's sending him these links?"

Jimmy took a deep breath and heard his chest rattle. His childhood asthma always threatened to come back when he was stressed. Script meetings weren't usually so stressful. It was normally one of the most fun parts of the film making process. Jimmy came up with ideas for the plot, Sam picked holes in them and they solved the problems together, throwing out all kinds of solutions and plot directions till they had the sucker nailed. It was how they always worked.

Only right now it wasn't working and they weren't enjoying it. They shouldn't have held the meeting at Sam's apartment, the place held too many recent memories.

"It doesn't matter."

"Of course it matters, it's a key plot driver. It's like having a murder mystery and never finding out who does the murder."

"But that's the point, you just said the key word."

"What key word—murder?"

"No, mystery, that's what make it so unnerving, the audience is never sure who sends him the links, we let them work it out for themselves, so they project their own fears onto it."

"How can they work it out if we don't know what's happening when we write it?"

"It's some unnamed supernatural agency then. Okay? Look you're getting bogged down in the details before I've actually given you the bigger picture. Just let me outline the story, alright."

"Alright, you're right I'm sorry. Go on." Sam held up his hands in apology. Jimmy cleared his throat, another indication of stress.

"So the guy's getting anonymous links to an underground darknet site."

"By guy you mean DC Harlow, right? The detective whose wife and child were burned alive."

"That's right."

"Very Derek Raymond."

"What?"

"The protagonist I mean, like the unnamed police officer who narrates all of Raymond's Factory novels."

"Oh yeah, yes, that's it exactly."

"So, these links take him to footage of a man being tortured to death, in some strange basement. The footage lasts about a minute or two and it's only live for five minutes, so he can't download it as evidence or anything. The torture gets more and more extreme and he's forced to investigate."

"Is he in vice or homicide?"

"Err . . . homicide, I think."

"So he's investigating murder, not snuff movies."

"Right, only he hasn't got any evidence because he's the only one who's seen the footage. So he decides to track down the guy in the video footage."

"How?"

"What?"

"How does he track down the guy?"

"He's policeman, he uses facial recognition software."

"Do they have that in the Met?"

"I dunno?"

"How does he use it if he doesn't have a picture of the guy's face? He can't download any of the footage remember."

"Oh yeah, well he uses a police artist to reconstruct the guy's face from memory then he goes through mug shots."

"So the guy in footage has a criminal record?"

"Yes, nothing too big, just petty theft or something."

"And just to be clear, this footage that DC Harlow is getting, that's the footage that we've got on the laptop right?"

"Yes."

"Okay, that can be edited in easily enough. We'll have to be careful not to show too much of their faces though."

"Right, back to the plot though."

"Sorry, go on."

Jimmy took a big pull on his latte and considered stopping for a cigarette. Probably not a good idea when his chest was so tight. "So, in the meantime, Harlow's contacted by this woman, a real looker."

"Strawberry blond?"

"Exactly, just like in the footage. So this woman, let's call her Nadine, she's been having these really vivid dreams, night after night, about someone being tortured to death in a basement. She's so convinced it's real, she goes to see Harlow about it. He asks her to identify the guy in her dreams and shows her some mug shots. She picks out the same guy he's been seeing in the darknet links."

"And these dreams she's having, that's more of the footage that we can splice in, right?"

"You catch on fast."

"Glad you notice."

"So now Harlow's got enough to go to his superiors with."

"Really? A bunch of dreams and darknet links no one else has seen? That's pretty flimsy evidence."

"Okay, well let's say his boss owes him a favour or two and he calls it in, in spite of his boss's scepticism. He tracks down this guy . . . "

"Finally."

"Shut up. He tracks down this guy to a dodgy cab office or something, only to find he's alive and well. Not dead, not tortured, not anything and not in any kind of trouble either."

"Right."

"So Harlow is hauled over the coals by his boss and we find out someone higher up in the Met has it in for him; the only person looking out for Harlow was his boss. If that's not bad enough, two days later the body of the guy in the footage turns up, obviously tortured to death. The footage was somehow predicting the future. Then Harlow finds himself in the frame for the murder."

"Why?"

"Why what?"

"Why would anyone think Harlow had tortured this guy to death?"

"Departmental corruption, someone upstairs has it in for him, like I said, and they find traces of his DNA at the scene, probably planted. So he's suspended without pay, pending a full investigation. Then, the same mysterious source starts sending links to his home computer. Once again it's footage of someone getting tortured to death in the same strange basement, only it's not just some random guy he doesn't know, this time it's Nadine who's getting tortured. Meanwhile, Nadine has been having more dreams too."

"Let me guess, she's having dreams of Harlow getting tortured to death."

"Yes she is. She's really freaked out about this, she tries to call Harlow but he's not at work."

'Because of the suspension."

"Yes, then she has an argument with her landlord and she gets kicked out of her flat. Harlow is really concerned about Nadine, all he wants to do is save her, but when he comes round to warn her about the clip, she's not there. The only way they have of warning one another is to locate the basement, the self-same basement that represents their future and the grisly fate that potentially awaits them."

"So how do they find the basement then?"

"I don't know yet. I haven't thought that far ahead."

"I thought you said you had it all sorted."

"I do have it sorted, I just gave you a premise, a concept and a way to use the footage cheaply and simply in a feature length film. It's got a central cast of three people with a few supporting roles and only four locations. What more do you want?"

Sam exhaled heavily and looked up at the ceiling. He didn't seem enthused.

"I dunno," he said. "It's all a bit . . . "

"A bit what?"

"It's all a bit . . . so what?"

"What's that supposed to mean?"

"You know what that means."

"I just don't get you sometimes. You've been difficult from the minute I got here. What is up with you at the moment?"

"I just don't understand why this Harlow is so concerned about Nadine towards the end?"

"Because of his backstory, because of the wife and kid that he lost. He wants to save her because he couldn't save them."

"Does loss make you fixate on things like that, on helping a virtual stranger?"

"No, but guilt can. If you feel you've let someone down badly enough, then helping someone who's in a similar predicament, even a total stranger, can make you feel better about yourself, even save you from yourself. It's about redemption isn't it?"

Jimmy ground his teeth and looked down at the floor. He realised his fists were clenched. He had a sudden mental image of Jennie. The way she used to tuck her hair behind her ear with her little finger when she was trying to concentrate on something. It felt like a blow to the solar plexus.

His breathing got faster. He looked up and caught Sam's eye. Sam read his expression straight away. "Mate, I'm sorry," he said. "I wasn't thinking."

"I need a cigarette," he said and stalked out onto the balcony.

CHAPTER SEVEN

JIMMY LEANED ON the balcony railing and gazed down into the canal as the final rays of sunlight fled the sky. He took one last drag of his cigarette and flicked the butt towards the towpath, admiring the sudden cascade of sparks as it hit the ground.

He needed Sam on board with this project. He couldn't let it go, not now. He had too much invested in it emotionally. He wasn't sure why it meant so much to him, but it gripped him like no other project before.

It wasn't just that it was going to be edgy and daring, walking that line between fantasy and reality, using footage of an actual murder. Making the viewer wonder how much of the torture is real. Few of them would realise.

He also felt there was an important statement to be made about the genre as a whole. This film was going to either damn or redeem him, both as an artist and a human being. This opportunity for salvation or damnation had a specific gravity, and Jimmy's soul was caught in its pull. Like the glowing end of his spent cigarette as it tore towards the towpath

He had to get Sam on board. He needed a hook. Something that would get Sam as personally invested as he was. He thought about Sam's reasons for making horror films. The things that drew him to the genre and made him such a passionate proponent. Then he recalled a conversation they'd had, shortly after they met in film school. They were round at Sam's apartment, hitting the bong, talking about the films they loved and the films they wanted to make.

Neither of them admitted to liking horror at first. It wasn't the done thing at film school. You had to pretend you were into Fellini, or arty 60s films like Antonioni's Blow Up and crap like that. The closest you could get to admiring anything that was actually enjoyable were Hitchcock's films. It was okay to say he was: 'a great auteur who transcended his sensational subject matter.'

Jimmy had mentioned Romero in passing and Sam had sheepishly admitted he had all his movies, even Survival of the Dead, which they both agreed was like an extended episode of The Walking Dead but with about a third of the budget. That opened the floodgates.

They both admitted to being hardcore horror fanatics. They'd watched so many of the same movies, some so obscure they couldn't believe anyone else had seen them. The discovery that they shared a love of the obscure and extreme was the foundation of their relationship. Jimmy had never worked so well with anyone, before or since.

That night, Jimmy told Sam he believed modern man finds things too comfortable and easy. "Too many of the everyday threats our ancestors used to face have been wiped out," he said. "But we haven't changed much as a basic organism. We're still hardwired for conflict and adversity, we just don't face it much these days, thanks to all our modern amenities. We still need someplace to channel those primal urges, that's what horror is for. I mean, I bet the stories that cavemen told around the fire were all about gruesome fights with cave bears or vengeful spirits and stuff. The ancient Greeks certainly liked a bit of gore, if I think back to my classics lessons."

"That's what I'm talking about," said Sam, putting down the bong and blowing out a big cloud of smoke. "The sort of people who think horror is little better than porn, are also the sort of people that think tragedy is the ultimate creative endeavour. What they don't realise is they're exactly the same thing. Tragedy and horror revolve around supernatural events, Hamlet sees his dad's ghost, Macbeth gets a prophecy from three witches, and Cassandra can see a dire tragedy for the future of Troy, but no-one believes her. And you're right, the ancient Greeks and the Jacobeans used to love their gore. Loads of blood was spilt on stage. They had special effects and everything."

"Like Hamlet stabbing Polonius in the arse?"

"That was an arras dumb-ass, but yes, that's exactly what I mean. Look at Euripides, too, Orestes killing his mother because she slit his dad's throat in the bath. Oedipus kills his Father on the way to Thebes, Medea murders Jason's sons because he cheats on her."

"Wait, Jason Voorhees had a wife and kids?"

"Fuck off, I meant Jason and the Argonauts and you know it."

"Now that was a cool film."

"Agreed, but the original Greek play was a hundred times more hardcore than anything Ray Harryhausen came up with. Tragedy has the same themes as horror, they're all about what happens when you challenge the natural order, or societal norms, or whatever. It always goes tits up, whether you're Doctor Faustus summoning demons or Mocata in The Devil Rides Out."

"They're both pretty fatalistic aren't they, tragedy and horror I mean."

"Yes, horror is the only modern genre that's as fatalistic as classical tragedy. But one is considered by critics to be the pinnacle of fiction and the other is considered the nadir."

"You know you get the cutest little furrow in your brow when you get all serious."

"Blow me," said Sam chucking a zippo at Jimmy's head.

"Only if you furrow your brow for me."

Jimmy took a hit from the bong and said, "You've thought quite a bit about this haven't you?"

"Yeah, I have. It means something y'know. The ancients used mythology as a way of exploring a lot of important, unspoken things about their lives. The closest thing we have to that is horror, it's our way of exploring the unspoken matters in life."

Looking back on the conversation, Jimmy was struck by how well Sam had summed up what Jimmy wanted to do with this project. As though he knew all along they were going to work on a film like this.

Something he'd read about Ancient Mesopotamia came back to him. He'd been doing some research on line the past few days. He hadn't thought, at the time, that it had anything to with the film, but he realised now that of course it did. Everything you read or watch, while you're engrossed in a project, ends up having something to do with it. At the time it feels like coincidence, but afterwards you realise it was fate.

Jimmy knew exactly how to get Sam excited about this film. He pulled open the french doors and strode into the living room.

"Have you ever heard of the ancient goddess Inanna?"

Sam looked up from the notes he was making. "Should I have?"

"You're about to," said Jimmy. "She was worshipped by the Sumerians more than five thousand years ago. She's also the subject of one of the oldest myths known to man."

"This is a bit left field."

"Actually it's not, in fact it's totally pertinent to our film."

"Okay, this I've got to hear."

"One of the oldest written stories in existence is Inanna's Journey to Hell, it's even older than the Epic of Gilgamesh. It tells how Inanna, a fertility goddess, travels into the afterlife . She descends through all seven levels of Hell, and then her sister Ereshkigal, an ancient, sex mad crone who rules the underworld, captures and kills her. Because she's a goddess she comes back to life and her lover, the shepherd king Dumuzi, sets her free. It's like the forerunner to lots of later myths about rescues from the underworld such as Orpheus and Eurydice, Demeter and Persephone and even this one Japanese tale, about the goddess Izanami-no-Mikoto and her husband Izanagi-no-Mikoto."

"Say that again."

"Izanagi-no-Mikoto."

"Fascinating."

"I know."

"I'm more blown away by the thought of you reading about ancient myths online. I didn't know you were into that sort of thing."

"I'm not normally, but that taxi driver got me thinking. Didn't you think it a bit weird that he just offered us that lift out of the blue, even though we were dripping with blood?"

"Not really, it's a cut throat business driving a mini cab. Some of those guys will give anyone a lift."

"But this guy was more like a mystic with all his talk about mysterious 'ancient beliefs' that are too old to have a name. I wanted to see if I could find out what he was talking about online. Ancient Mesopotamia is like the cradle of civilisation, it contained one of the oldest organised religions in history."

"But what does any of this have to do with the film?"

"What if Nadine is a professor of Sumerian culture. Let's say she's studying a bunch of cuneiform tablets, that's how they used to write things down in those days."

"Yeah, I know, on little clay tablets. Cuneiform is the oldest form of writing we know about. You're not the only one who watches the Discovery Channel you know."

"Okay, glad to see you're keeping up."

"So these tablets tell the myth of Inanna, only it's not a version anyone's read before. It's an older one that's even more gory."

"Is this Inanna myth a gory one then?"

"Oh man, it's the original splatterpunk. If you think

Greek tragedy is a blood bath, wait till you hear about this. When Ereshkigal captures Inanna, she impales her on a spike like that infamous scene in Cannibal Holocaust."

"The one where they find the native girl with the stake up inside here and coming out her mouth?"

"Yeah, only Inanna is a goddess and doesn't die easy, if at all. Plus she has her guts hanging out and spends all her time screaming out to the other gods how much her entrails hurt."

"Seriously?'

"Seriously. I looked it up in whole load of places. Anyway, maybe it's the tablets that trigger her prophetic dreams and she becomes convinced this basement she sees in her dreams, where all the tortures occur, is part of the ancient Sumerian underworld. The myth starts repeating itself. Nadine is possessed by Inanna and taken to the underworld so Harlow has to take on the role of Dumuzi to come and rescue her."

"So everything that happens is like a reoccurrence of this ancient myth cycle."

"Exactly."

"Or, as our mini-cab driving friend would have it, the Inanna myth is the really old story that lies beneath the surface of our new one."

"Totally, now you get where I'm coming from."

"So how does it end?"

"I told you, I haven't worked that out yet."

"No, not our story, this Inanna myth. I was thinking if we know how that ends, maybe it'll give us an idea of how to end our film"

"I didn't actually read that far," said Jimmy,

stroking his beard. "I've got no idea how it ends. But you're right, I'll do some reading up before we start the script."

"Great."

"That's exactly where we should look for help with the ending though. You know how you've always said before that horror is like a modern myth, a contemporary equivalent to ancient tragedy? Now you've got a chance to work on a film that really makes that clear. This film could say something about the meaning and purpose of horror, do you get me?"

"I'm beginning to."

"It covers every aspect of the genre, from the worst excesses of modern snuff, to the ancient roots of horror in the mother of all myth cycles. This is our grand statement about the state of our art form. Are you in on this?"

Sam smiled and nodded his head. "Okay," he said. "You sold me. I'm in."

Jimmy sighed with relief. "Thank fuck for that."

"Of course our biggest problem now is going to be casting."

"Do you think?"

"Definitely, where are we going to find a strawberry blond that's a match for the one in the footage?"

"Oh, I've got a pretty good feeling about this. I'm pretty sure someone will turn up."

CHAPTER EIGHT

IMMY HATED AUDITIONS. They were an exercise in mutual humiliation. You sat behind a rickety table, in a musty rehearsal room, and pretended to be interested in the resumes of a dismal procession of drama school drop outs, who pretended to be interested in your film.

Because it was an Indie horror film, none of the agents they contacted sent their brightest or best. The guy they'd just seen had nothing but extras work on his resume. The highlight of which was a Swedish advert for haemorrhoid cream in which he'd been: "at the front of the queue of people who pushed their way out of the lift at the end." This gave him a "full second close up in the lengthier cut." The saddest thing was that, although abysmal, he wasn't the worst person they'd seem that day.

The next two actors pulled a no-show.

"Maybe that's a blessing," said Jimmy. "Let's just knock it on the head and go down to the pub."

"No," said Sam, ever practical. "We'll give them ten more minutes then we'll go over the resumes again. I'll contact a few more agents and we'll do another round of auditions."

Jimmy threw himself back in his chair and groaned. "Okay, if you insist."

That's when she walked in.

Jimmy sat bolt upright. She walked up to the rickety table and placed her hand on it. Jimmy had never felt envious of an inanimate object, until now.

She had strawberry blonde hair, high cheekbones and the sort of full lips that looked moist no matter what make up she wore. She was wearing a pair of faded men's jeans and a baggy Tommy Hilfiger t-shirt, neither of which hid her curves or the relaxed sensuality of her walk. Only her pale blue eyes belied this sensuality. They were full of pain, the sort of pain only a saint or a martyr ought to know. Jimmy didn't know why, but he instantly felt protective of her.

"Is this where the auditions are?" she said.

"That's right," said Jimmy.

He and Sam exchanged the same surprised look. It wasn't that she'd appeared out of nowhere. Nor was it the way she seemed to dominate the space with her presence alone. It was the fact that she was identical in every way to the woman in the footage. They could have been separated at birth. Hell, they probably were.

She was carrying a handful of black and white photos. She put them on the table and sat down without being invited. "I'm Melissa, these are my head shots."

"Melissa . . . ?" said Sam glancing through his list, fishing for her last name.

"That's right," she said, without giving it. "So this is going to be a horror film, right?"

"Yes it is. Melissa, I don't seem to have you down for an audition. Who sent you?"

"Oh no one. When I found out you were doing this auditions, I thought I ought to drop in."

"How did you find out about them?"

"You can never keep these sort of things secret, you must know that."

"Indeed."

"So is it going to be a 'found footage' film?"

"Erm, what makes you say that?" said Jimmy.

"Just about every horror film is these days isn't it? I thought it was the vogue."

"There is going to be some . . . err, footage . . . which we did find, but we're going to go for a mix of styles."

"Sounds interesting."

"Have you had much experience in front of the camera?" said Sam.

"Well, I'm probably the only actress in London who hasn't done an episode of Casualty. Though I think I could play a really good victim, don't you?"

You don't know the half of it, thought Jimmy.

"Would you mind doing a camera test?" said Sam.

"Not if you were behind the camera," Melissa replied, leaning forward and looking Sam right in the eye, head tilted, a single finger resting on her chin. An intense intimacy passed between them that made Jimmy furious. It was typical of Sam, who only thought with his cock when it came to actresses.

"Of course, we must impress our director here," she said turning towards Jimmy, her hand stroking her chest, her lips curled in a provocative smile. Jimmy felt the sweat break out on the back of his neck. "You are the director aren't you? You look as though you have a talent for it."

"I, err . . . oh, yes, I erm, write and I direct."

"We both write," said Sam. "It's a collaborative effort." Jimmy caught his eye and saw the same envy and resentment on Sam's face as he'd felt a moment ago.

Melissa sat back in her chair and Sam and Jimmy leaned forward in unconscious unison. "I have a few conditions if I'm going to work with you," she said. "I can't work with more than one person on the set. That means no cast, no crew, just me and the person behind the camera, that's all."

"That's going to make directing you a bit difficult," said Jimmy. "Not to mention recording sound and dialogue with the other actors."

"I'm afraid it's a deal breaker for me. Think of it as a challenge. I'm sure you have more than enough talent to work around it. Oh, and you can't phone me and I don't have any internet. You'll have to tell me where and when each shoot is going to take place when you see me beforehand. Shall we start the week after next?"

"Well I haven't actually worked out a shooting schedule yet," said Sam. "We've still got to finalise the script . . ."

"Let's say Thursday the thirteenth then."

"Erm, okay . . . can you make an eight o' clock call?"

"I'll be there at ten."

With this Melissa got up and walked to the door. "Wait," said Sam. "We don't even know the location of the first shoot. How will you know where to go?"

"Oh, I found you once. I'm sure I can find you again." She shot them a smile that made their fillings ache and slipped out of the room.

Jimmy let out a deep breath. Sam shook his head in disbelief.

"What the fuck just happened?" he said.

"I think we just found our leading lady."

"Seriously, just like that?"

"She's perfect. You saw her, she's a dead ringer for the woman in the footage. She could be her exact double."

"But we don't know anything about her. We're not even certain she can act."

"C'mon, after the performance she just put on, I think it's safe to say she's a natural."

CHAPTER NINE

"HERE HE IS," said Alfie, as Jimmy walked into the tiny front room of Alfie's council flat. "George Jung, famous coke smuggler."

The comment was a reference to the real life character Johnny Depp played in the film Blow, one of Alfie's favourites. It was also a dig at Jimmy over the coke deal, that had gone spectacularly wrong.

"More like cock smuggler," said Tim, a tall fat bloke with a huge beard, who took up more than half the sofa he was sprawling on. He was usually round Alfie's when Jimmy called.

"Or cock juggler," said Alfie. He was a short guy, no more than five foot five, with dark hair, shaved at the sides. He had a Cypriot look on account of his Greek dad and spoke in a broad east end accent. He was also an inveterate gossip and sold the best blow in North London. Nothing went down north of the river that he didn't know about within hours, even though he hardly left his high rise flat.

Jimmy had a ton of things he'd promised to do that day. He also had five large in his pocket from a quick job as camera man on a corporate video. So his first order of business was procuring a few grams from Alfie.

"D'you think they'll make a film about dickwad here?" said Tim, shifting onto his sizeable left buttock so he could fart.

"Dunno," said Alfie. "But they wouldn't call it Blow they'd call it Blown It, innit."

"Very funny guys," said Jimmy. "But I nearly got killed, thanks to you."

"What's that s'posed to mean?"

"Well you introduced me to Ashkan."

"I set you up with a backer for one of your films. Someone who was gonna lend you a shitload of money, with no interest, so long as you gave him a part, that's all. And did I get any thanks? Did I fuck. I didn't tell you to spunk all his dosh on a dodgy fucking drugs deal now did I?"

"I guess not."

"Course not, so don't come pissing and moaning to me about it. You're just lucky things turned out the way they did."

"What do you mean?" said Jimmy, turning suddenly cold.

"What, you ain't heard? Thought you'd be made up."

"Heard what?" Jimmy was struggling to keep the frustration out of his voice. He knew Alfie would only wind him up more if he spotted it.

"Well you know Charlie McKenzie's been looking for him."

"No!" Jimmy was startled. He didn't know many people in the criminal underworld, just his drugs connections and the few criminals he'd met through them, but everyone had heard of Charlie McKenzie. He was one of the most feared crime lords in the city. He had his hand in everything from drugs to prostitution.

"Fuck me," said Alfie, half annoyed. "You don't know nothing do you? I don't know why I bother telling you anything if you can't keep up."

"But why is Charlie McKenzie after Ashkan?"

"Why d'you think, you dozy bleeder? Why does anybody go after someone. For money, 'course."

"Wait, Ashkan owes money to Charlie McKenzie?"

"Quite a lot by the sound of it. Not been paying his dues or summink. Anyway, the important thing is, Ashkan's done a bunk innit."

"He's disappeared?" Jimmy tried to sound as surprised as he could without over egging it.

"Totally," said Alfie. "And not just Ashkan, his whole crew too. No-one's seen hide nor hair of 'em in days. Charlie's boys have turned over his house, his office his crash pads everything and they haven't found a fucking thing."

"What about the lock up in Bethnal Green? He showed us it once, said we could film there."

"Oh that, they cleaned that right out, didn't find jack."

"What, no blood or nothing?"

"Didn't I just say they found nothing? Are you even listening to me? Why would they find any blood?"

"I dunno, I just thought . . . maybe there'd been a gangland killing or something."

"Gangland killing, fucking listen to him." Aflie shook his head and sneered.

"Yeah," said Tim. "Maybe he's worried they'll find out he rubbed 'em all out."

"That's right," said Alfie. "Regular fucking Lepke B this one, one man Murder Inc."

For a second, Jimmy was back in the lock up with

the piles of shredded flesh and blood dripping from the ceiling. He couldn't understand how all that could have gone by the time Charlie McKenzie's men turned up. Did someone come and clean the place up?

Jimmy felt a sharp pain in his side. He turned and saw Alfie had punched him.

"You even listening to me?" Alfie said.

"Sorry," Jimmy said. "I've got a bit on my mind."

"I said are you here to score or what?"

"Oh yeah right."

Jimmy pulled out a wad of notes and practically threw them at Alfie. He grabbed the ziplocked baggies of powder that Alfie produced, and headed straight for the door. It seemed that all trace of the massacre had disappeared. Jimmy had to speak to Sam as soon as he could.

"See you then, you rude bastard," said Alfie, as Jimmy slammed the front door behind him.

CHAPTER TEN

HE STUDIO THEY were renting was on the top floor
of a converted warehouse by the river. Sam was
with Melissa, filming the scenes where she, as
Nadine, was alone in bed, dreaming of torture in a
dingy cellar. Jimmy wondered what Melissa would
think if she could see the footage they were going to
splice in as the dreams she was having? He guessed
she would see some of it eventually, just not in its
current form.

Sam and Jimmy hadn't finished the script yet, but
they'd worked the bedroom scenes into shape. Those
seemed the best things to shoot first. They both agreed
it was the easiest way of breaking Melissa into the
project.

Neither of them was sure she was going to show as
they waited for her that morning. They'd had no
contact with her since the audition, nearly three weeks
ago. She did turn up though, and only twenty minutes
late. She'd been firm about keeping to her condition of
having only one person on set with her at a time.

She'd chosen to work with Sam that day. Jimmy
wasn't quite as bothered by this as he might have
thought. He was almost relieved to leave her alone
with Sam, though he wasn't sure why. There were a ton

of things he had to do, and it had given him a chance to go and score from Alfie, something he felt a pressing need to do.

Jimmy loitered in the courtyard when he arrived, smoking a couple of cigarettes. Sam wasn't due to wrap for another half an hour, and Jimmy didn't want to disturb him, even if they needed to talk pretty urgently. To take his mind off what he'd learned at Alfie's, Jimmy tried to think of creative ways to get around the conditions Melissa had set. He wasn't sure why, or even when, they'd agreed to these conditions.

They'd have to shoot all her scenes twice, film her dialogue in close up, then use a stand in, shot from behind, when they reshot the scene with Harlow, who they still hadn't cast. Jimmy kept thinking there was a clever way to get round this challenge. Some brilliant technique or concept he hadn't thought of yet. But, for the life of him, he hadn't come up with it yet.

Maybe he needed a little powdered inspiration. He had three baggies of it burning a hole in his pocket. It wouldn't hurt to nip up to the first floor toilets and do a couple of lines. He still had some time to kill before Sam and Melissa were done.

Jimmy bounded up the stairs to the first floor landing where the toilets were. He had his head down, so he didn't realise there was anyone on the landing until he collided with them.

"Hey, I'm sorry," he said, then looked up to see Melissa, hand on her chest, smiling with surprise. "I didn't realise you were done already. I didn't hurt you did I?"

"I'll live," said Melissa. She tucked her hair behind her ear with her little finger in a way that was alarmingly familiar.

"Look," Jimmy said, suddenly awkward. "I'm not checking up or anything, I mean we're sticking to your conditions and everything. I was just waiting to see Sam when you wrapped."

"That's alright, I saw you out of the window, down in the yard. Sam was setting up another shot, so I asked if we could finish for the day."

"Why? I mean we're on a pretty tight schedule."

"I don't want you to think that I prefer Sam to you, just because I asked him to film my segments."

"What? Oh no, don't be silly. I never thought anything of the . . . that is I know your request is erm, unconventional but y'know we're all professional here."

"Good, because I don't prefer him."

"Of course not, I never imagined you, erm . . . "

"In fact, I'm not sure I could trust myself if we were alone for any length of time."

Jimmy felt the sweat break out along his back. Melissa stepped a little closer and his heart rate soared. He could smell her perfume, sandalwood, incredibly evocative, old memories stirred in a dark place at the back of his mind. Someone, very close to him, had also worn sandalwood.

Melissa seemed to change as she leaned into him. Her eyes were downcast and her mood suddenly solemn. She looked up at him gravely and said: "I can trust you can't I?"

"Trust me? Of course . . . of course you can."

"If anything were to happen, to me that is. I could count on you."

"Melissa, are you in some kind of trouble?"

Melissa looked away, her eyes seemed about to tear

up. "No, it's nothing, I'm sorry, I'm just being silly. Forget I said anything."

"I'm sure you're not being silly. You can tell me, I won't judge, honestly."

Melissa put a hand over her mouth and blinked to stop her eyes watering. She was gathering herself. "Okay," she said. "It's just this myth, the one my character's studying. I was thinking about Dum . . . er . . . "

"Dumuzi."

"That's right, I was thinking about how he goes to Hell for Inanna and . . . well, oh God, you're going to think me really foolish."

"Of course I won't."

"It's just that I've known a lot of men you know."

"I'm sure you have."

Melissa blushed, suddenly coy. "That's not always a good thing, I mean they all promise you the world, but they never deliver. And I know Inanna's a goddess and all, but this Dumuzi was only a man and yet he still went to Hell for her. I can't think of any man that would do that for me."

"I find that hard to believe."

"You don't know the men I've known. They're not all like you."

Now it was Jimmy who blushed.

"Would you . . . I mean . . . no, this is crazy. I've only just met you," she said. "I shouldn't be asking this."

"No, that's okay, I don't mind."

"So you do care a bit about me?"

"More than a bit."

"You're not just worried about your film?"

"I'm always worried about some film or other. That

doesn't mean I won't help if I can. But you do need to tell us if anything is going to affect the shoot."

"If I wasn't here you'd look for me wouldn't you? You'd try to find me. Like Inanna, you'd be my Dumuzi wouldn't you?"

"I'm not sure I follow you? Why wouldn't you be here? Is someone threatening you?"

"What I'm trying to say is, you will come for me won't you? Promise me you'll come back for me and not leave me too long."

The memories began to stir again, like rats under a nest of newspapers in the dark cellar of his mind. They broke free and swarmed into his thoughts. It wasn't just Melissa's scent, it was more than that.

In an instant he was back by the side of that road five years ago. Jennie had just stepped out of his car. She was hugging herself agains the cold and drizzle, smiling with hesitation and apology, her pupils huge from all the E she'd taken.

What Melissa had said was uncanny. Those were Jennie's very last words to him, before he left her at the side of the road and headed back into town. Her exact last words.

The loss Jimmy felt, whenever he thought about Jennie, came flooding back. It was like a sledgehammer to the chest, knocking the breath out of him. He was never going to see her again, never going to hold her, never tell her how sorry he was.

If Melissa noticed the effect her words had on Jimmy she didn't show it. She just slipped past him and headed down the stairs. She turned back to him when she reached the bottom.

"That's a promise now, isn't it, Dumuzi?" she said.

Jimmy nodded, his breathing still shallow, his feelings too intense to process.

As soon as the door slammed shut, Jimmy came back to himself. What the hell was Melissa playing at? Did she know what effect those words would have on him? Did she know about Jennie, had Sam mentioned something to her? Jimmy tore down the steps. He was going to confront Melissa and find out what her game was.

He tore open the front door, only seconds after it had shut. There was no sign of Melissa, she'd vanished. A lady in her late thirties stood a few steps from the door. She was wearing a cardigan with a cami and a pair of worn jeans. She looked very confused.

"Where am I?" she said.

"Riverbank Complex, on Wharf Road," Jimmy told her. "Have you taken a wrong turn?"

The woman looked right through him, as if she hadn't a clue what he was saying.

"What time is it?"

"Around half three," Jimmy glanced at his watch. "Listen, you didn't happen to see the woman who just left this building did you? Slim, curvy, strawberry blonde hair."

The woman gazed around her and shook her head in disbelief. She didn't seem to have heard a word Jimmy said. She wandered away from him in a daze. Her dishevelled state, her confusion and vulnerability all reminded him of Jennie.

He closed the door gently and laid his forehead against its cool metal. He would never get over Jennie. Guilt and recrimination welled up inside him like an angry geyser of bile. He wanted to move on, to put the loss behind him, but he felt too guilty, as though he still deserved to suffer.

He couldn't cope with these feelings. Not now. He had to self-medicate. He headed straight to the men's room and chopped himself a massive line.

Say what you like about Alfie, he sold the best blow in North London. Jimmy's nose and throat, even his front lip, were numb from the stuff. His synapses burst into life like the grand finale of a firework display. He was sharper now, more focused and more creative, able to knock this film into shape.

More importantly, a glacial sheet of ice had crept over his emotions, numbing them all. This was why he stopped smoking weed and switched to blow. The crippling pain of remembering became a manageable throb, a dull ache he could live with.

Melissa had caught him off guard with her perfume. Total coincidence it was the same as Jennie's. So she'd repeated the last thing Jennie ever said to him, it wasn't an unusual phrase or anything, anyone could have said it. He was still a bit stressed about the incident with Ashkan, that's all. Having Alfie go on about it had put him on edge.

He took a deep breath, checked himself in the mirror, left the toilets and headed up to the studio.

CHAPTER ELEVEN

SAM HAD TAPED signs saying: 'QUIET PLEASE—FILMING IN PROGRESS' all along the corridor and also at the entrance of the studio. Gone were the days of a red or green light over the door. Even though he knew they weren't filming, Jimmy still entered tentatively.

Down the opposite end of the studio was the bedroom set Jimmy had helped Sam build and dress over the past couple of days. Furnishing it as cheaply as possible, from charity shops and market stalls. He had to admit Sam had done a great job of lighting it.

Sam was in a different part of the space, standing over the makeshift desk they'd set up. It was covered with recording equipment and several laptops. Sam was staring at one of these laptops, frowning over the footage he'd just shot.

"So how'd it go?" Jimmy said. "Melissa any good?"

"She's okay," said Sam, after a long pause. "Nothing special in the way of talent."

"Really? That's a surprise. Her looks though, she's perfect for the part. So long as she's not embarrassing we can fix everything in the edit."

"She's not embarrassing, I'll give her that. There's an issue with the camera though, the one we . . . y'know

. . . acquired. I think it's the one they used to shoot the footage we saw."

"Really, that's kind of freaky. Gives us a bit of an edge though. Could be good for the production."

"Possibly. It must have some kind of setting that I don't know about. I can't work out how to turn it off."

"What do you mean?"

"Do you remember how there was some kind of filter that obscured the guys who were doing the torture?"

"Yeah, made them all blurred and shadowy, have you worked out how to do that?"

"Not yet, but that's how Melissa came out on the film. Everything else in the frame is perfectly in focus, all apart from her. There's even a moment when it looks like there's been a double exposure."

"A double exposure?"

"Yeah, like there's someone else in the shot, like Melissa's been superimposed onto another woman, it's only for a couple of frames but it's totally inexplicable. Never seen anything like it before."

For a moment Jimmy thought of the lost and confused woman in the courtyard, but that brought back more memories of Jennie, so he banished her from his mind.

Jimmy sighed. "So we can't use anything you shot today?"

"Doesn't look like it."

"There's a way around this." Jimmy's brain was whirring. He could fix this. "That weird effect looks pretty spooky. We drop little jump cuts of the stuff you shot today, between frames, when we want to get all atmospheric and it'll help us build to the big climax when the blurry shadows get to work."

"Maybe."

"What do you mean maybe. Have you got a better idea?"

"I guess not. It's kinda strange though. It's why I didn't mind so much when she suddenly took off, out of the blue."

"Yeah I heard."

"When did you hear?"

"Well I . . . err, ran into her on my way up."

"Oh. She wasn't pissed off about you hanging around then? Didn't think you were breaking one of her conditions?"

"No, not at all. Listen, you didn't say anything to her about erm, Jennie or me did you?"

"No, why on earth would I bring that up?"

"I dunno, it's just . . . well she said something a bit weird about me coming to find her if she went missing."

"What's that supposed to mean?"

"Your guess is as good as mine."

"She's not going to pull a no show on us is she? Look what happened last time. We lost over a week off our schedule when the cast went awol."

"It wasn't that bad, it was only one girl who blew us out. And you have to admit we treated her pretty rough. She thought it was gonna be all glamorous, fresh out of drama school, looking for her first film break. Instead she spent the day naked, covered in blood, being stabbed by a guy in a Justin Bieber mask."

"Yeah, and the time we lost recasting and reshooting is why we were so over budget. We can't let that happen this time. We've only got these premises for a short while. We can't afford any more if she disappears."

"She's not going to disappear okay, don't sweat it. She was just acting a bit intense and dramatic. You know what she's like."

"Yeah," said Sam, nodding but not really listening. He was concentrating on the camera and rewinding what he'd shot that day. Jimmy wondered if he should press Sam anymore about the weird coincidence and his memories of Jennie, but thought better of it. Sam was uptight and freaked out enough as it was.

Then he remembered why he'd torn round there. "Listen, I went to see Alfie earlier today."

"I can tell."

"What's that supposed to mean?"

"Well, you're a tiny bit nasal, and it's too early in the year for your hay fever."

"Fuck you. Anyway, that's not important. You know how Alfie likes to bust everyone's balls, well he was trying to mug me off about this business with Ashkan, then he tells me something really weird."

"What was that then?"

"Well it turns out Ashkan's into Charlie McKenzie for a serious amount."

"What, the Charlie McKenzie?"

"The very same, and his men have been looking for Ashkan all over."

"In all the wrong places."

"No, it turns out they went over every inch of the lock up. Tore the place apart. Didn't find a trace of Ashkan, or his crew."

"What about all the minced up bodies."

"Gone, all of 'em."

"How'd that happen?"

"You tell me."

"The guys who killed 'em, must've come back and cleared up. Do you think we're in any danger."

"No, why should we be?"

"What if those guys think we're witnesses?"

"Then they'd have killed us on the day. We obviously don't count to 'em, we're not part of that world."

"But we've got a film of them murdering three people."

"It's probably not even them, it was someone else Ashkan pissed off. Besides, even if it was them, why would they care? That special effect they've used, the one you haven't worked out yet, means they can't be identified anyway, so it doesn't matter. If it did, they'd have taken the footage before they left."

"Maybe you're right," said Sam, sitting down and breathing a long sigh. "But I still think we're in over our heads."

Jimmy didn't say anything. He knew Sam was thinking about the pools of blood and how they seemed to get smaller every time you glanced at them. He knew Sam thought something was amiss, so did Jimmy, and he knew that no amount of coke would freeze that out.

CHAPTER TWELVE

"RIGHT," SAID JIMMY, bounding back into Sam's living room. "Let's get this script treatment sorted."

There were coke crumbs around his left nostril. Sam knew he thought the stuff made him more creative, but it also make him a bit of an arsehole. Especially if they were under pressure to finish something. It was already late, and they had to be up early tomorrow to prepare for another day of shooting.

"What we really need to work out is how the whole story wraps up. Did find out how that myth ends?"

"Not yet, I'll get around to it later."

"I thought you said you were going to read up on how it ended before we started the script."

"I don't know if you've noticed, but I've been a little busy of late."

"It's just that it might help us come up with a conclusive ending," said Sam. "Something that will tie up the whole plot."

Jimmy frowned. "Does it have to be totally conclusive?"

"Yes, we don't want to cheat the audience."

"We're not cheating them if we leave the ending open. It's okay to let them do some of the work themselves."

"You always want to leave the ending open. And what does that mean anyway, letting 'the audience do some of the work themselves?'"

"It means they piece the story together themselves. We don't spoon feed it to them, they have to work out what happened from all the clues we leave them."

"But we're not leaving them any clues and how can they work out what really happened if we don't actually know ourselves."

"Look, it's like Sacheverell Sitwell said . . . "

"Not this old quote again, you got that from Cold Hand in Mine. I read Aickman too you know."

"Good for you, doesn't mean it doesn't bear repeating. 'In the end it is the mystery that lasts and not the explanation.'"

"Why can't we just have a proper ending for once?"

"Neat endings kill the mystery. Explanations are for Scooby Doo. 'Look kids don't be scared, it wasn't a zombie, it was just Mr Jones the janitor trying to scare people away from his goldmine.' Once you explain something it stops being scary, because the biggest fear, like Lovecraft said, is fear of the unknown."

"But Lovecraft had great endings," Sam said. "And none of them were open ended."

"You're missing the point—again! If you tie things up neatly at the end you let your audience off. If you kill the monster at the end of the movie and restore the world to how it was, then Mr Moviegoer and his date leave the monster right there in the cinema. If you leave a bit of doubt in their mind, then they take the monster home with them. It's still lurking out there in the car park, or under their bed, waiting to strike them at any moment."

"But there aren't any monsters in this movie."

"Stop doing that."

"Doing what?"

"Taking everything I say literally. The monster is a metaphor okay, a metaphor for horror. I want the audience to bring the horror home with them."

"I'm sorry, I'm just not buying it. I've seen too many arty horror films and read too many short stories that ended inconclusively. They don't scare me, they just leave me dissatisfied and annoyed that I've wasted time and money on them, when they couldn't be bothered to tie up all the loose ends."

"But the best work being done in the genre, the really important stuff that's getting proper critical acclaim, all of it gets the audience to do the work for themselves. That's how you know it's clever and not just some pulpy, exploitation piece."

"That's just a current fad, it's not a sign of quality. What's so clever about letting someone else do all the work for you. You don't get conductors at the proms passing the baton over to the audience. When did Hendrix ever invite someone else up to play his guitar solo for him? When someone starts asking me to do some of the work for them I want some of my money back. If I want to do the work myself, I may as well write my own story. That's why I got into films in the first place."

"Now you're just being an arse."

"I'm being an arse?"

"Yes, quite frankly, you are mate."

Sam sighed. 'Okay, sorry, you're probably right. We've neither of us had much sleep lately, and we've both got stuff to do tonight. Like tomorrow's dialogue for one."

"Leave that with me."

"Okay, can we strike a compromise? How about we find a way to tie up the loose ends without actually ending the story?

"I'd like to see you try," said Jimmy. "If you can do that, I'll move into the story myself and become the lead character."

"Careful what you wish for."

"What's that supposed to mean?"

"You've seen enough horror movies, you know what happens when you say things like that."

"Ooh, going all meta on me now, are you?"

"Maybe," Sam rubbed his eyes, they were sore and tired. "Look, I'll see you tomorrow early, okay?"

"Okay, I'll just phone for a taxi."

CHAPTER THIRTEEN

THE NEXT MORNING they waited for Melissa. They got in early, as planned, and re-dressed the set so it would now work as a living room. Jimmy had stayed up all night writing dialogue and Sam had edited it that morning.

By midday there was still no sign of her. "She's not coming," said Sam, obsessively retying his man bun. "I fucking knew it!"

"Relax," said Jimmy. "She'll turn up."

But she didn't, not that day, nor the next.

"We're fucked," said Sam, on the third day. His eyes were red and his chin unshaven. Sleep had evaded them both the past few nights. Sam had even dipped into Jimmy's coke stash, something he rarely did these days. "We haven't got an ending, we haven't got a cast and we haven't got our leading lady anymore."

"We can fix this," said Jimmy. "It's alright, I'll find her."

"It's not her you should be worried about, it's our whole fucking film."

"But I am worried about her," said Jimmy. "I am."

CHAPTER FOURTEEN

JIMMY'S PHONE BUZZED as he turned off Oxford Circus into Berwick Street. It was Sam.

"Any sign of her?" said Jimmy, hopefully.

"Nope, this is the fourth day she hasn't shown up. I told you she's not coming back. We're pissing away money here, money we don't have. We need to regroup, come up with a new plan and hold some more auditions. And we need to do it now. No more wild goose chases."

"Just let me chase down this one last lead."

"Listen to you, when did you become Sam Spade?"

"Fuck off, I think I'm finally on to something."

"We can't find her, just admit it. We've been through every single headshot on spotlight.com, contacted all the agents we can think of, looked at every actor's directory there is. There aren't any other leads. We need to start focusing on the project otherwise it's gonna go tits up."

"Look I know you're right, but let me do this one last thing. I got out some old copies of Spotlight from the local reference library this morning, from before they put it all online. I found her mate, I finally found her."

Sam sounded cautious. "Okay, well done, but did

you get any contact info? I'm guessing most of it will be out of date by now."

"I got her old agent's number."

"Did you call?"

"I did, but they've moved since. I left a couple of voicemail messages on their new number but they haven't gotten back to me, so I'm going to doorstep them."

"You know, even if you do track her down, there's no guarantee it'll help us. There's a reason she pulled a no show and most likely it's because she doesn't want to be involved anymore. That's just a fact we need to face now."

"I know, I know, but just let me do this one last thing okay?"

"What is it with you and this girl?"

"I think she might be in trouble, I think she wants me to help her that's all."

"Well, I hope you know what you're doing. I hope you're not going to jeopardise the whole project because of this."

"Of course not, you know what this film means to me."

"I do, I hope. I'll make a start on editing down that footage until you're back. In the meantime I'll wait for your call shall I?"

"Definitely, I'll phone you in a couple of hours, see you."

"See you."

Sam rang off first. He hadn't sounded too pleased with Jimmy, but then he hadn't been pleased with much the last three days.

Jimmy negotiated the maze of backstreets that led

to the agency's office. Soho had seemed like such a dangerous, exciting place when Jimmy was a teen.

Back then it was filled with strip joints, porn shops and back street brothels. Now it was luxury apartments for Russian and Chinese billionaires. He guessed the mini cab driver would have said the old Soho was still there underneath all the new developments, you just needed to know where to look. Funny how a random conversation with a total stranger can stay with you sometimes.

After a few wrong turns he found the address. The agency's name, BTSD Talent, was next to one of the buzzers on the intercom. Jimmy pressed it.

"Hello," said a female voice.

"Yeah, I'd like to see Janice Strang, please," said Jimmy. The person he was speaking to hung up on him.

Jimmy buzzed again. "Err . . . hello . . . I'm here to see Janice Strang."

"Do you have an appointment?"

"No."

"You need to ring and make one."

"I did ring several times but you never got . . . " She hung up on him again.

Jimmy swore, took a walk down the small street then back up again. He pushed the buzzer again. When the receptionist answered this time, he put on a deeper voice and said: "Got a package for Janice Strang, needs a signature." The receptionist buzzed him in and he walked up to the tiny fourth floor office.

"Look," Jimmy said, as the receptionist, a bored girl with bright red, hair, looked for the package. "I'm not a courier, I'm actually a director and I need to speak to your boss."

"If you're really a director, what are you doing here?"

"Well now, this may sound a bit novel to you, seeing as you handle actors and all, but I need to speak to your boss about someone she represents. Someone I've employed in my current film."

"Why didn't you make an appointment?"

"Well I would have made an appointment if you'd actually answered your phone or returned my calls, instead of forcing me to come see you."

The receptionist looked at Jimmy with blank expression. He could see that she didn't believe him. He looked about the cramped office. It contained two other desks, both empty, but piled with papers. At the back was a wooden door that probably led into another space. On the wall, next to the girl's desk, a series of head shots had been tacked up under the heading 'AWARD WINNERS.' Jimmy recognised one of them.

"Look," he said. "That's the actor David H. Church right? The only award he's ever won is a Damnie, that's a Best Damn Horror Award, and he won that for his part in My Brother's Creeper,' a film I directed." The receptionist continued to stare at him. "If you don't believe me, pull up his file on your computer."

The girl tapped at her keyboard for a minute then looked up. "It says here 'My Brother's Creeper' was directed by James Walden."

"That's me," said Jimmy showing her his driver's license and hoping at the last minute she wouldn't see the coke crumbs down one edge of it. She did, but weirdly that was probably what convinced her he was telling the truth.

She got up grudgingly and popped her head around

the door at the back of the office. After a brief but muffled exchange she came back to her desk. "Ms Strang says she can spare you five minutes, but no more."

CHAPTER FIFTEEN

THE BACK OFFICE was even smaller than the front one, with just enough room for a small desk and two chairs. Jimmy had to close the door before he could sit down. Janice Strang was a hard bitten, middle aged woman with dyed, brunette hair, an expensive manicure, and just the right amount of make-up.

"I wasn't aware I'd placed anyone with your project, Mr Walden."

"Call me Jimmy. And I'm not actually here to talk about an actor you currently handle. It's one you used to manage."

"Oh," said Janice, already losing interest.

"Her name is Melissa Scott."

Janice looked up from the papers she was sorting with a shocked frown. "Mr Walden, if that's who you really are, I don't know what your reason for coming is, but I find that in very poor taste and I don't wish to continue this conversation. Kindly see yourself out."

Jimmy was so surprised by this response he got out of his chair, then sat down again and said, "Wait, did you have some sort of problem with Melissa. Does she owe you money?"

"Mr Walden, you know full well what happened to Melissa."

"No, no I don't. Please, if something has happened to her you've got to tell me. It could be important. We've got a very tight schedule and she hasn't turned up for the past three days. We're haemorrhaging money we don't have from the budget."

"Melissa Scott disappeared over two years ago under very suspicious circumstances. I can't see how she could possibly be in your film."

"But she is, she turned up to the audition like she already had the part and started making all these conditions before we'd even offered it to her."

Janice removed her Armani spectacles and massaged the bridge of her nose. "What sort of conditions?"

"She said she'd only work with one other person on the set, no cast or crew, just her and the DP, that's the director of photography."

"I know what DP stands for."

"And she wouldn't give us any contact details. She'd set her own calls, turn up when she wanted."

"That certainly sounds like Melissa. She wasn't a particularly gifted performer, but she had a certain look that you directors seem to like. She could have worked continually if she didn't keep making all these demands. It made her impossible to manage and I had to let her go in the end."

"You mentioned something suspicious about her disappearance?"

"Nothing was ever proven, but there were a lot of unsavoury rumours."

"What sort of rumours?"

"She moved in some rather strange circles and kept some pretty wild company. There was talk of her getting caught up in some underworld drug war. She was in the wrong place at the wrong time with the wrong people. I heard she was kidnapped and tortured along with two other men, all very distasteful. There was even talk about them being in a snuff film."

"A snuff film?"

"Yes, surely you know what one of those is, in your line of work?"

"I know what a snuff film is. Everyone knows what a snuff film is. But I mean . . . it's never been proven that they actually exist."

"And there's no proof that this film actually exists. Like I said it's just a nasty rumour. There were a lot of rumours attached to her disappearance. She was that sort of girl."

"This isn't making any sense, if she disappeared, if she was . . . killed or something, how could I have seen her, spoken to her?"

"I have no idea."

"She didn't have a sister or anything did she? I mean like a twin or something?"

"She had a sister, but not a twin so far as I'm aware. In fact, that reminds me. The family got in touch with me several times. I should give you their number. If Melissa really has turned up again, you should let them know."

Janice pulled out her phone and wrote the number on a sticky note. James stood and went to the door in a daze. "Listen," he said. "Thanks for seeing me."

"I'm not sure I was of any help to you, but good luck with finding Melissa. If it is Melissa you're looking for. She was always a bit of a lost cause that one. A regular damsel in distress if you catch my meaning."

"Erm, right."

Jimmy left the office and made his way back down to the little side street. Night was drawing in and the shop fronts and cafe windows of Soho took on a garish and unreal cast. The shadows seemed too sharp and the streetlights threw down an unnatural glow.

Things were starting to make less and less sense. Was this snuff film Janice mentioned the footage he and Sam had? Had Melissa somehow survived it? Jimmy hadn't actually watched the part where she was killed yet. He'd had his eyes closed in the lock up. Was Melissa massively scarred under her clothes? Was that why she wouldn't let anyone else on set?

Jimmy shuddered when he thought about her turning up to star in a film that contained scenes of her actual torture. How had she found out? Was it the people who'd killed Ashkan and his crew? Had they sent her? Was she trying to escape them, was that why she wanted him to come find her? He should probably try at the very least. He owed her that much.

Jimmy felt as though he'd stepped over some unseen threshold into a world that was entirely outside his understanding.

CHAPTER SIXTEEN

SAM STOOD UP, closed his eyes and massaged his temples. He wondered if the work would be any easier if he were stoned, or did a couple of lines? Probably not, it might even make him worse.

Only H, or crippling amounts of alcohol, could make him numb enough him to deal with the footage, and he didn't like either of those highs;, certainly couldn't work on them. It wasn't just the extreme images that were getting to him, it was also his Mac. It kept playing up.

As he'd promised Jimmy, Sam was using the dead time to edit the footage, taking out the worst bits and preparing clips to splice into the film. He was working in the studio space. They'd already rented it and he might as well put it to some use. Plus he was reluctant to work on the footage in his home. As stupid as it sounded, he was afraid it might taint his apartment.

It had actually taken him a while to build up the courage to go through the footage. Every time he viewed it he was back in the lock up, taped to a chair, powerless. Sam hated feeling powerless; he boiled with rage every time he thought about it. How dare they do that to him. Then he thought about what had been done to them, their blood congealing on the concrete floor, and he hated himself for letting any of it happen.

Finally, he was so sick of swinging between anger and self-loathing, he sat down at his Mac.

"Fuck you," he told the footage. "Fuck you, you do not get the better of me. I'm in control now, you are my bitch!"

Of course the footage had other ideas. For a start his Mac kept playing up. He couldn't seem to get an accurate cut of any clip he wanted. No matter how careful he was with the tracking, when he saved a clip and played it back, it showed something else. It either started a minute late, or it showed some detail he hadn't seen before. It felt like a big digital maggot, pinned to a slide, that kept squirming every time he tried to cut it, making it impossible to dissect.

Sam's eyes hurt and there was a painful little knot right between his shoulder blades. He was tired, not just from lack of sleep, but from fighting to keep the film afloat when he should have let it sink days ago. Costs were spiralling, cast members were awol and they had no workable script, or even an ending. Too many things were just going wrong on this film.

Sometimes you have to cut your losses before you find yourself in over your head. Working on the footage reminded him it was real people on those operating tables. Real people suffering unbelievable pain and violation. He and Jimmy were planning on exploiting them for commercial gain. What sort of person makes money out of other people's murder?

He and Jimmy apparently.

It had seemed really edgy and intense when they'd first come up with the plan, but now it seemed kind of desperate and seedy. Sam might well have been one of those victims himself. If Ashkan hadn't been killed, it could have been Sam strapped to one of those tables, screaming and begging for his life.

He wondered how he might feel, if he knew in those last moments that people would be paying to watch him die. Getting a cheap thrill out of seeing him at his most powerless and vulnerable, as everything that made him human was slowly stripped away from him. He shuddered as he pictured this, then he hung his head and nearly wept from the deep shame he felt. There was no way he could work another minute on this project.

Perhaps it wasn't just the project he needed to abandon. Maybe Sam needed to pull out of Indie Horror altogether. He wasn't thinking about putting on a suit and tie and becoming a stock broker, but there were other things he could do in film.

The thought surprised him. He'd always gone all out for horror and considered himself a 'lifer' in the business. There'd been a time when horror had saved his life, or it had felt like it at least.

He'd been very anxious as a kid. It hadn't helped that his parents shipped him off to boarding school as soon as he was old enough. He'd started wetting the bed at prep school and suffered recurrent panic attacks. He wasn't good at sports, and hated the long hours he was forced to spend on muddy playing fields, so he had nowhere to put all his nervous energy. For a while he even developed a few tics, which made him a target for bullying.

In his last year of prep school he'd been walking through the local town, when a group of boys jumped out at him from a shop doorway. It was the town's only second hand bookshop. The boys, from the year below him, were holding horror books in front of their faces. One showed a green looking mummy's head, another had a werewolf on it, and the third had a photo of a human skull peering out of a semi melted snowman.

The boys came at him roaring and howling as children do when they pretend to be monsters. Sam stood still and stared at them, bemused and slightly embarrassed by their behaviour. When they saw that their little prank had failed to scare Sam they threw the paperbacks at his head and ran off.

The owner of the shop, a tall, bald man who wore a tweed jacket with patches on the elbows, burst out of the door and shouted after them, but the boys just laughed and gave him the finger. Sam was still standing in front of the shop so the owner rounded on him.

"What do you think you're playing at you bloody little savages?" said the owner. Sam couldn't think of a single things to say; he just stared nervously at the man.

"Well you're paying for those books," the owner said. "And any other damage you've done."

Sam picked the ancient, battered paperbacks off the pavement and saw, for the first time, they were part of the Pan Book of Horror Stories series. He was an obedient child, so he dutifully got out his weekly allowance, but he couldn't believe how much the owner was asking for them.

"They're collectors' items now," the man said. "Go and check on your interweb thingy if you don't believe me."

Sam put the books into his bag and slunk back to school. With no money left to spend, he didn't feel like hanging around in town.

He felt extremely furtive when he snuck back into his tiny, windowless room with the books. A month before, three boys had been suspended for keeping porn mags in their room. Sam was a timid boy, and he wondered what his housemaster would do if he found Sam with these gruesome looking books. He imagined the look of shame and disappointment on his mother's face if he were to be suspended. Sam slipped all three books into the gap between the back of his wardrobe and the wall, hoping no one would think to look there until he could get rid of them.

A week later Sam was confined to his room with a severe chest infection. He couldn't go to lessons and he wasn't even allowed into the common room to watch TV in case he infected someone. All he could do was finish his schoolwork and stare at the walls. After two days of high temperatures and intense boredom, he remembered the three books.

Sam pulled out the one with the Mummy on the cover, because it looked the most innocuous. It was entitled the Ninth Pan Book of Horror Stories. He wasn't the least bit prepared for what he found inside. The first three stories involved emasculation, murder and burning at the stake. In his fevered state Sam felt he was not only watching the characters' suffering, he was experiencing it along with them. He flung the book at the wall and then hid it again, wishing he could burn it like Jinnot, the young girl in the third story who was burned alive.

Something about the plight of the innocent girl had

affected Sam though. He identified with her on a deeper level and that released some of the nervous tension he kept bottled up. Later that night he dug the book out again and finished it by torch light. Before he recovered he'd read all three books twice over and had become an irredeemable horror fan.

After that, Sam spent every penny he had on DVDs, novels, and back issues of Fangoria, the more extreme the better. Horror gave him a place to put all his anxieties and fears, as well as a way to control and exorcise them. He lost his nervous tics, stopped getting bullied and took up running when he moved to his senior school. He never joined the popular crowd, but he managed to survive boarding school, and whenever things got a bit much, there was always horror.

It was horror that toughened him up and helped him cope with his problems, not team sports or cold showers. People often spoke disparagingly about the way horror desensitises people to violence and atrocities. Sam thought they were completely missing the point. That's what horror was supposed to do.

The world, as he saw it, was a very violent and atrocious place, and horror was his way of inoculating himself against that. By exposing himself to controlled doses of violence and psychological fear, he was able to build up a greater tolerance to it. It was the emotional equivalent of a vaccine, or snake charmers taking small sips of snake venom till they're immune.

The natural conclusion to this was to start creating his own horror, to find a place to put all his personal demons, and that's what he and Jimmy had done for the past three years. Now it was time to stop.

Sam had witnessed genuine torture and had very

nearly suffered it himself. In the face of that, horror didn't seem so exciting anymore. The idea of covering some actor in fake blood, and filming them scream with a pain they'd never actually known, all seemed rather pathetic.

Maybe that's why he'd liked Jimmy's idea of pushing the envelope with real footage, but the implications were too terrible to contemplate. Sam felt like he'd just stepped back from a huge abyss. He knew, with a sudden certainty, that he would not have been able to live with himself if they'd completed this film.

He had no idea how he was going to break this to Jimmy. He was effectively dissolving the partnership with his best friend. It needed to be done though, otherwise he'd grow to hate the medium that had done so much for him.

A huge knot of tension slipped from the muscles between Sam's shoulders. This was an important decision and a necessary one. He let out a deep breath, surprised by how emotional he felt.

Sam bent over his laptop, quit Final Cut Pro X and dragged the files he'd edited out of their folder to bin them. He was about to do the same with the footage when something stopped him. He let the little icon hover over the trashcan and then he pulled it away. He didn't know why, but he wasn't ready to get rid of it yet.

Strangely, he still wanted to watch it to the end. In fact, the idea suddenly excited him. He wasn't sure why. Maybe he wanted to see how desensitised he'd actually become, to test the limits of his endurance. Or it could be the fact that he finally had a choice about watching it. He wasn't obliged to view it because of work, or forced to watch it by some homicidal loan shark. He could regain control of how he felt about the whole thing.

He was tremendously relieved about letting go of the project and he fancied a little thrill, to watch it for the sheer experience. It was also a way of empowering himself. Sam had been feeling powerless a lot lately, in the face of his treatment by Ashkan and his inability to keep the film on track. Maybe this footage was just the thing he needed.

Sam liked all kinds of horror, but he did have a bit of a thing for extreme slashers and torture porn. If he was honest, he always identified with the tormentor, not the victims. Leatherface, Jigsaw and Michael Myers were gods. Who wouldn't want to have naked teens cowering at their feet. The thought made Sam feel powerful and it also kinda turned him on.

The footage was like the ultimate torture porn. It would be his final indulgence, his good bye to the genre. Going so far into the dark stuff that he'd never want to go back.

Sam sat down, opened the file and set it to full screen. It seemed to start slightly differently. There were details he'd over looked before. He was probably viewing it with a clearer mind, he told himself, the trauma had blotted those things out.

He was wondering about pausing the footage and getting a beer when he felt a hand on his shoulder. He swung round to chew Jimmy out for sneaking up on him, when he looked up into two pale blue eyes. Eyes that contained equal amounts of suffering and sensuality.

"Melissa," Sam said getting to his feet. "What are you doing here?"

"I thought I was starring in your film."

"So did we, until you disappeared."

"I'm sorry." Melissa dropped her chin and looked up with a penitent pout. She put a finger lightly on his chest and traced his collarbone. "Are you very cross with me?"

Sam pulled away, sighing heavily. "I was, up until about ten minutes ago. Then I realised this whole project was a mistake. We shouldn't have started it in the first place. I'll pay you for today and the other day you worked, and maybe one more day, but that's all I can afford to be honest."

Melissa continued to regard him with those pale blue eyes. Sam found it hard to read her expression.

"I'm sorry if that's a let-down," he said. "I didn't think you were coming back. Thought you'd found a better project or something."

"You haven't let me down. I need you and Jimmy. I can't tell you how, just yet, but I do. Where would I find a better project than this?"

"Just about anywhere. The pay isn't great, the hours are long and what we had planned . . . " Sam let his head drop with sudden embarrassment. "I don't even want to tell you what we had planned."

Melissa put her hands under Sam's chin and tilted his head up so he was looking her in the face. "You know how you make God laugh don't you?"

"No?"

"Tell him what you had planned."

Sam laughed. Why was she trying to cheer him up when he'd just fired her?

He found himself looking at her mouth. Her lips were full and moist and quite perfectly pink. They parted in a subtle pout, as if they were reaching out for him. Sam wanted to know what it would be like to feel those lips brush his, to have them touch his skin and part to receive his . . . No, he really mustn't go there. He was just torturing himself.

"The only thing I'm really going to regret," Melissa said, leaning in closer. "Is not spending more time with you. Just the two of us, alone together here."

Melissa was so close Sam could smell her scent, sandalwood and fresh broken sweat. Was she really coming on to him? That was impossible wasn't it? Girls as hot as Melissa didn't come on to guys like him. He'd worked with some good looking girls and they were occasionally flirty, but that was just part of the job. They never meant anything by it.

Melissa leaned in to him. Her stomach pressed against his and he could feel her nipples hard against his chest. Oh God, maybe she was coming on to him, but why?

Should he really be worrying about that right now? This was a once in a lifetime opportunity, did he really want to mess it up?

Oh God what if he couldn't perform. She was so gorgeous it was intimidating. If he failed to rise to the occasion Sam didn't think he could stand the humiliation.

Melissa put her hands on Sam's shoulders and tilted her pelvis so it was pressed against his crotch. That's when Sam realised he would have no problem rising to the occasion. He was so hard he was about to pop the stitches of his 501s.

Sam put his hands on the small of Melissa's back, feeling clumsy and hesitant, but so desperate for her he was shaking. Melissa pressed her cheek to his and ran her fingers along his shoulders.

Sam's breathing quickened, he was swaying and stoned on his desire for Melissa. He wanted so badly to kiss her but he didn't want blunder into it. Was she waiting for him to make the move? How could he do it without making an idiot of himself.

She moved her cheek gently along his, bringing their lips closer together. My God this was it.

The jarring roar of an angle grinder whined out from the laptop on the desk. Melissa and Sam turned towards it at the same time.

Shit! Sam had completely forgotten about the footage.

He was so surprised by Melissa's entrance, he hadn't turned it off. It was still playing!

CHAPTER SEVENTEEN

THE CAMERA MOVED from the first victim to the woman on the operating table. The one who was identical to Melissa. As the blurry figures went to work, she looked heavenward with eyes every bit as blue as Melissa's.

Oh shit. Oh no. What was she going to think of him now?

Melissa hands fell from Sam's shoulders to his waist as she leaned over to get a better look at the screen.

"Look, Melissa, it's not what it looks like," Sam said. "Okay, it is what it looks like and I know what you must be thinking, but I swear to God I was just about to . . . "

Melissa put a finger to Sam's lips. "Shh," she said. "We're missing the best bits."

"What?! You're not . . . ? I mean, I thought you'd be like . . . livid."

"What I am is wet. And this film just makes me wetter." Melissa ran her fingers over Sam's crotch. "I notice our friend here has gotten a little shy. I do hope he's going to put in another appearance." She stroked Sam through the front of his jeans, coaxing him back to life, looking at the laptop all the while with a weird hunger in her eyes.

Melissa took hold of his jeans and undid the buttons. She pushed him back into the chair then knelt and pulled down his jeans and boxers. Sam glanced over at the laptop. "Want me to turn that off?" he said.

"Don't you dare," a strange avarice shone in her eyes.

What kind of person gets off on watching a snuff film where their exact double is tortured to death? Sam would have been pretty freaked if Melissa's expert fingers hadn't found his cock. Stroking it and massaging the sensitive little ring of flesh just beneath his helmet.

Melissa bent forward and blew on the end of his cock, her perfect lips almost touching him. She looked up, caught his eye and chuckled. The chuckle was echoed by the girl in the footage. Only it wasn't so much an echo as a simultaneous occurrence, like they were in synch.

For the briefest time, Sam thought he saw someone else kneeling in front of him. As though Melissa was superimposed over them, the same as the single frame of the footage he shot. Then it was gone and it was very obviously Melissa in front of him.

Before Sam had time to dwell on this, Melissa gently teased back his foreskin and ran her tongue around the exposed helmet, licking up a little bead of pre-come. Sam closed his eyes and let his head fall back as the pleasure her tongue brought spilled down through his loins and travelled as far as the soles of his feet. When she finally put those wonderful lips around him, and took him in her mouth, it was so intense he nearly sobbed with relief.

Her lips gripped him lightly, moving up and down

just as expertly as her fingers. Her tongue circled his helmet, stroking the rim where he was most sensitive, making his pelvis shake with every flick of her tongue.

Sam could feel the orgasm building like some immense pressure that threatened to propel him out of the chair. He didn't want to come so quickly. He opened his eyes and glanced at the laptop to distract himself. To his surprise, the girl in the footage appeared to be sucking one of the blurry figures. It was hard to tell because the figure wasn't in focus. Sam couldn't remember seeing this before, but then, he'd been trying not to look at this point.

The footage had the effect he wanted and he pulled back from his orgasm. The head of the girl in the footage seemed to be keeping perfect time with Melissa as she took the blurry member in her mouth, which was kind of eerie, even if it was a coincidence.

Sam closed his eyes again, he didn't want to spoil the enjoyment. So Melissa was into some freaky shit, who cared when the head was this good. Melissa pulled her mouth away and Sam felt so bereft he let out a high pitched sigh. Way to go macho man.

"How about a little deep throat," Melissa said, and Sam was certain he could hear the woman on the footage saying the exact same thing, but he must be imagining it. He nodded, breathing hard, eyes still closed, not trusting himself to speak.

Sam felt himself swell as he slipped down Melissa's throat. A warm trickle of saliva spilled out over his scrotum. Melissa tightened her throat muscles and Sam groaned. This was incredible.

He'd had deep throat only once before, from some actress he'd met at a party, but it was nothing like this.

Basically she'd just swallowed him and he couldn't really feel anything apart from her lips around the base of his cock.

Melissa was massaging the whole of his shaft by contracting her throat muscles. It was unbelievable. Every one of Sam's nerve endings lit up. He didn't think he could take much more without some release.

Oh God, please don't let me come, he thought.

Please don't let me come, not now.

More saliva spilled out, trickling down his bare thighs. Sam didn't think he could contain himself. He opened his eyes and saw that on the video the shadowy figures were slicing open the woman's windpipe.

Sam turned away and looked down at Melissa. She smiled back up at him.

Wait a minute, smiled back up at him?

Yes, smiled. Her chin was resting on his abdomen. Her beautiful lips were drawn back in a smile that showed perfect white teeth and her pale blue eyes sparkled.

But he was still inside her. He could feel her throat working him.

Melissa lifted her chin off Sam's abdomen and pulled her head back. Then he saw that it wasn't saliva spilling over his balls, it was blood.

Sam's cock was stuck in a ragged hole in Melissa's throat. The same ragged hole that the woman in the footage had.

"What the fuck?" he cried. "What the . . . what?"

Melissa continued to smile as she grasped his cock at the base and squeezed tight, applying pressure like a cock ring so he didn't lose his erection. She pulled her throat off him and shifted her position so that she was straddling him.

Her breathing was a hoarse rasp, blood bubbled and frothed at the corners of the wound. Thick, red rivulets ran down her chest and over her breasts.

Keeping one hand on the base of Sam's cock, Melissa lifted her dress with the other, she wasn't wearing any underwear. She lowered herself onto him.

If anything, Melissa's internal muscles were more deft than her throat. She gripped him, warm and wonderfully moist, taking him even closer to orgasm.

Sam couldn't bear to look at the blood gushing from her throat. He turned to the laptop and saw the figures inserting a large, sharp blade, like a broadsword, into the woman's crotch.

Blood poured out over Sam's lap, hot and warm, as Melissa continued to ride him. More and more of it came with every thrust of her pelvis, pooling round his buttocks, soaking into the fabric of the chair and dripping into the boxers and jeans around his ankles.

"No, don't," he said. "Please don't. Stop it, please just stop." He didn't want this. He didn't want this at all. He just wanted her to stop, to get off him and leave. But she didn't. She held him inside herself, deeper and deeper and he couldn't do anything to stop her.

Melissa put her left hand up against his mouth to silence him. Sam turned his head away. She pushed three fingers between his lips, penetrating his mouth as she forced him to penetrate her.

On the footage Sam saw the figures take a large pair of shears to the woman's same three finger. Sam felt his mouth fill with blood.

Melissa pushed Sam's teeth apart with bloody stumps as her severed fingers filled his mouth, threatening to choke him.

No, no, no! he thought.

Melissa pushed herself harder against him, took Sam to the very brink of an orgasm he didn't want, not now, not like this. It wouldn't be right. He screwed his eyes shut and willed himself not to succumb.

Oh God, please don't let me come, he thought.

Please don't let me come, not now.

CHAPTER EIGHTEEN

COURSE, HACKNEY'S NOTHING like it used to be," said the Big Issue vendor, as Jimmy fished around in his pocket for change. "Ten years ago it still had an edge. You could get all manner of dodgy goods from the market. And the squat parties, that's what I miss the most, them and the crack dens with the boarded up windows. All these yuppies who've moved in, they've fucking ruined it."

"A wise man once told me it's still all there," said Jimmy. "Underneath the surface of the city"

"The fuck's that supposed to mean?"

"How should I know, I've never driven a mini cab." Jimmy handed the guy his money and headed off down the street still smiling.

The house he was looking for was in a little cul de sac, off the Lower Clapton Road. It was one of those Victorian terraces that were popular round these parts. It hadn't been renovated, as so many of them had. Melissa's sister Suzy had told him where to find it.

Incense and patchouli wafted out as she answered the door. Suzy was shorter than her sister and a bit thicker round the waist. She was a good seven or eight years older than Melissa, wearing a long ethnic dress and jewellery with lots of magical symbols. She had the same blue eyes and strawberry blonde hair, only hers was grey round the temples. She was obviously related to Melissa, even if she wasn't as attractive.

"It's Jimmy isn't it?"

"That's right, Suzy, yeah?"

"Yes, come on in."

She led Jimmy into a small front room that looked like a cross between a Victorian parlour and a Moroccan tent. There was a battered chest of drawers and an antique tall boy but no chairs or sofas. The floor was covered with middle eastern rugs and cushions with a low table in the centre.

"That's William Blake isn't it?" said Jimmy, looking at one of the prints on the wall.

"Yes it is."

"But who did these two?"

"Austin Osman Spare, he was a visionary artist and a magician, a bit of a genius actually. He knew Aleister Crowley, but they didn't get on very well."

"Oh."

"Would you like some tea?"

"Yeah, that would be great."

"Have a seat," said Suzy, indicating the floor. "I'll be right back. Earl Grey okay?"

"Fine."

Suzy returned with a tin tray containing a chipped brown teapot and two mugs. She handed Jimmy a mug with a picture of the Cabalistic tree of life on it.

"So you're into all this magical stuff then?" said Jimmy. "Being a medium and all?"

"I study the occult because the world I live in isn't like the world everyone else inhabits. I see and hear things they don't."

"Like dead people and things?"

"I inherited the gift from my mother. It runs strong in our bloodline."

"Does that mean Melissa has it, too?"

"Melissa chose to do other things with her talents, but yes she too is . . . I mean was sensitive to the spirit world."

Jimmy sipped his tea, it was hot and he slurped louder than he meant to. He smiled apologetically at Suzy who was regarding him with such intensity he felt naked. More than naked, it was as though she could see beneath his skin.

"You said you had some information about my sister's disappearance."

"That's right, well to be honest, it's more to do with her reappearance."

"Reappearance?" Suzy held up her hand and turned suddenly to look over her shoulder, as if she'd just heard a noise. "I'm sorry, you said reappearance, that's not possible, she's dead."

"You're the second person who's told me that, but I've seen her, I even employed to work on my -"

Suzy held up her hand again and looked back over her shoulder. "Look will you please be quiet, this is important and I need to listen."

"Are you talking to me?" said Jimmy.

"No, there's someone else here with us." Suzy inclined her head, as though she was listening to someone, and frowned. Jimmy felt a little embarrassed. He wasn't used to eavesdropping on a conversation where he couldn't see both participants. It was like watching someone argue with their imaginary friend.

"I'm sorry Jimmy, but she insists on talking to you."

"To me?"

"Yes, she's wants to know why you didn't come for her, why you left her so long?"

Jimmy swallowed, but his mouth was very dry. When he spoke it came out more as a croak. "What do you mean?"

"She's about five foot three . . . sorry five foot five . . . with long straight hair that's a sort of reddish blonde, it looks dyed . . . okay sorry, it's natural actually . . . alright, will you stop . . . yes but will you stop . . . look you have to stop correcting me so I can talk to Jimmy. She's wearing an old leather jacket with badges on it and she says her name's Jaime . . . no sorry, well speak more clearly . . . it's Jen . . . Jenny. Do you know a Jennie? with an 'ie.'"

"Fuck Off!" Jimmy got to his feet, surprised at the violence of his response. "No!" he said. "I'm not one of your gullible, fuckwit punters. I don't know how you found out about this, but you're not pulling this Derek Acorah shit on me."

Suzy frowned and lifted her chin. "I'm not trying to pull anything on anyone. You came to me claiming to have information about my sister and then you tell me she's reappeared, even though I know she's dead. If anyone appears to be pulling anything, it would be you."

"How do you know she's dead, you can't know that."

"I felt her when she died. We were very connected. I could always read her thoughts, or tell when she was coming to visit, or just about to phone. It's something everyone in our family can do."

"That's ridiculous, no one can really do that."

Suzy turned to talk over her shoulder. "Look, can you just stop for a minute please . . . he's not listening . . . I don't care, I don't think I want to talk to him if he's going to use language like that." She turned back to Jimmy. "I'll tell you what's ridiculous, turning up at a complete stranger's house, telling them you just employed their dead relative then swearing at them. So I think you ought to leave."

For some reason this panicked Jimmy. Even though he didn't want to believe what Suzy was saying, he didn't want to leave yet.

"No, look, I'm sorry," he said. "You just shook me up with what you said. You don't know, you don't know what it means."

"That's okay. Nonetheless, I'd like you to go."

Suzy took him gently by the shoulder and led him out into the hall. Suzy moved her head and spoke over her right shoulder. "That's enough, I'd like you to go, too. This conversation is over . . . okay . . . okay . . . I'll tell him. She says it was a blue transit. She says they did stop. She heard a door open, but they drove straight off. It took her a little while to die and she never stopped hoping you'd come back."

Jimmy heard a high pitched wail, followed by coughing sobs. He wondered who was making such a ludicrous noise and then he felt his chest shake and he knew it was him. He slid down the hallway wall and curled up like a foetus.

He hadn't cried at the funeral. He hadn't cried when Jennie's mum had thrown her drink in his face at the wake, telling Jimmy it was his fault because he led her daughter astray. He'd been dry eyed through the bleak months of depression when he'd remained locked up in his room and had to get a deferral on his course. But something inside him just gave way and he couldn't deny the tears any longer.

At some point Suzy must have gotten him up and back into the living room, though he wasn't aware of this. He was aware of the new tea she poured him and the strange one sided conversation she kept up.

Then, just as Jimmy was composing himself, Suzy said: "She's gone." Jimmy felt so bereft that he lost the ability to cry.

"You mean she's gone towards the light or something?" he said.

"No, that's not how it works. That's just Hollywood rubbish. I think she was actually a little scared by how you reacted. To be honest, so was I."

"I'm sorry, I've never, I mean I haven't ever . . . I . . . That's the first time I've let it all out. I've been holding on to it for so long. Shit, she was really here wasn't she?"

Suzy nodded.

"And I fucked up, again. I scared her off, and now she's gone and I can't talk to her." Jimmy held his head in his hands as an immense pressure seemed to build at the back of his nose and eyes. It was as though all the regret he felt, and all the things he wanted to say to Jennie, had focused themselves into one painful spot behind his face, like a logjam of emotions.

He was breathing too hard, his chest was tightening and his head swam. Suzy placed a calming hand on his shoulder. "Calm, okay? You need to breathe more slowly. Why don't you talk to me about Jennie. Did you know her long? She was involved in some sort of accident wasn't she?"

Jimmy nodded. He slowed his breathing, then began to tell Suzy what had happened five years ago.

He'd been seeing Jennie for nearly a year and a half. They'd met when she was a freshman and Jimmy was in his second year. He was pretty sure Jennie was the one, though he couldn't help wondering what he'd miss, being with the same person for the rest of his life. He'd only had two other sexual partners and he was still determined to live a wild Hollywood lifestyle one day.

All the same, they couldn't let a day go past without spending all their free time together. He needed to be around her, even if she was just in the room while he finished an essay, or worked on a script. It was like a physical ache, and the sex was the best he'd ever had. Jennie watched way more porn than him and had a wild imagination.

They were coming back from a warehouse party when it occurred. Jimmy was driving his beat up Toyota Avensis. Jennie was next to him and Benny was in the back seat. Neither of them really liked Benny. To be honest, he was a bit of a douche. The kind of guy who thought humour was belching in someone's face or pissing in their can of lager while they were out of the room. He needed a lift though and he was seriously out of it. Benny's friends were worried about him, so Jennie'd offered him a lift.

He looked pretty ill when they left the party, and he started to go in and out of consciousness on the way home. The last time he came round he admitted he'd had a pretty strong dose of smack. It was obvious he'd taken too much and was beginning to OD.

If they didn't get him to a hospital he was going to

die. Jennie didn't think she could face a hospital though, not in the state she was in. She'd taken some heavy duty E and the come down was rough, so she'd smoked some skunk and was feeling paranoid.

Benny went grey and his eyeballs rolled up into his head. Jimmy knew that if they didn't get him to the hospital he was going to die soon. They had to turn round and go into the city right away.

The out of town campus, where they were both living, was just over half a mile away. Jennie told Jimmy to drop her off and she'd walk back along the little country roads. She made him promise to come back and pick her up as soon as he'd dropped Benny off.

The last thing she said to him, as she stepped out of the car and hugged herself against the cold and the rain was: "You will come for me won't you? Promise me you'll come back for me and not leave me too long." She'd smiled with hesitation and apology, her pupils huge from all the E.

Jimmy took Benny to A&E, but it had taken forever to get him seen and he died before the doctors could help him. Jimmy had to fill out forms and answer all sorts of questions, and then the police were called. It was early morning before he got away and he went straight to his room and crashed.

It wasn't till he woke, late the next afternoon, that he went to call on Jennie. She wasn't in her room and no-one in her halls had seen her. He asked all over campus but no-one knew where she was. The next morning Jimmy put out an alert and the police were called. The roads around the campus were combed and Jennie's body was found in a ditch under a hedge.

There was no verge where she was found and she'd turned a blind corner in the dark just as a vehicle was coming round it. The coroner said she would have died soon after the impact. The driver who hit Jennie was never identified.

Jimmy knew who was really responsible for Jennie's death, though. He was. He'd put Benny before her, even though the guy was an asshole. He should have dropped Jennie safely home, not left her to walk. He should have gone back for her, not wasted time in the hospital.

Benny was dead from the moment he took that smack, but Jennie wasn't. It was Jimmy's fault that she was walking that road when the van hit her. He shouldn't have let her do it. He should have made her stay in the car. He shouldn't have wasted his time trying to save someone who was as good as dead. He tried to help the wrong person and lost the woman he loved.

The recrimination bubbled up inside him like a poisoned spring that seemed incapable of running dry. His whole body was heavy with it. Suzy listened politely, then went to make more tea.

"I'm sorry you didn't get to chat with Jennie," she said.

"It's my fault I guess. I wouldn't let her speak. She accused me of the same thing while she was alive."

Jimmy got to his feet. "Look, I'm sorry to have bothered you, I really don't know what I was thinking. You're right, I should go."

CHAPTER NINETEEN

WAIT A MINUTE," said Suzy. "You came here with information about my sister. I'd like to hear it now."

"Why now?"

"You may not realise it, but your aura's changed. When you came here your colours were guarded, deceitful and conflicted. The crying and the confession have opened you up, something's been unlocked, your chakras are more in synch. I think you should tell me what you know."

"You don't really believe all this new age claptrap do you?"

"And here we are back to being cynical, in spite of what just happened. You're not fooling anyone you know. This isn't the only weird thing that's happened lately is it?"

"You couldn't possibly know about that."

"Know about what?"

"It doesn't matter."

"You say you employed my sister, was this recently?"

"Yes, we're supposed to be shooting now. That's why I've been looking for her, she's disappeared again. We're losing money on the shoot and . . ."

"Yes?"

"Well she asked me to come and look for her, if something like this happened."

"Really?"

"Yes, in fact the last thing she said was: 'you will come for me won't you? Promise me you'll come back for me and not leave me too long.' Which is also the last thing Jennie said to me."

"And then Jennie, makes herself known to me, the minute you call."

"Well you are a medium, that must happen a lot."

"Not out of the blue like that. Usually it takes a while if I'm with a client. I have to make myself properly receptive. They're not usually so loud and insistent."

"Do you think there's a connection?"

"I don't know. How did you come to meet Melissa?"

"She just turned up at the auditions, she didn't even say how she found out. She wasn't on the list."

"And you didn't think that was strange?"

"Everything about her was strange, no offence, but you must know that, she's your sister."

"And yet you gave her the part."

"Well she didn't really give us any choice. Besides she was perfect."

"In what way? She wasn't a particularly talented actress."

"She just had . . . how did her agent put it . . . the right look."

Suzy stared a few inches above his head. "You're keeping something from me," she said.

"What are you implying?"

"I'm not implying anything. Just stating a fact. Your crown chakra is out of alignment and there's a black and red pall over your aura. That means you're lying. And before you accuse me of using new age bullshit, you also looked up and to the left as you spoke and you touched your nose, two classic psychological tells."

"Yes, alright, we've all seen Lie to Me."

"You do know you could be in danger don't you? I know how Melissa comes across, I've seen her femme fatale act myself, many times, but she ran with some really wild crowds. Some of the people she hung out with were beyond hardcore."

"So, I know some pretty wild people myself."

"Not like these people you don't."

"What, a bunch of violent drug dealers? You should see some of the people who back our films."

"I'm not talking about petty criminals, I'm talking about immortals and fanatical heretics."

"Now you're sounding like a Hammer horror movie. What immortal heretics?"

"Ever heard of a Mr Isimud?"

"The guy who shot the . . . I mean, yes, someone mentioned him to me recently."

"I'm impressed, what did they say about him?"

Jimmy shrugged. "Y'know, stuff."

Suzy rolled her eyes. "Did they tell you that's who Melissa was looking for before she died? That she was studying the Qu'rm Saddic Heresy and . . ."

"Studying what?"

"The Qu'rm Saddic Heresy, I doubt you've heard of it."

"Is it anything like 'The Oldest Truth,' or 'The Faith that Came Before Man?'"

Suzy looked at him with genuine surprise. "Yes, those are other names for it."

"What does that have to do with this Isimud character?"

"It led her to him and she became certain he could give what she most wanted?"

"Which was?"

"Immortality."

"Like fame you mean, her name living on after she was dead?"

"No, I mean real immortality, living forever without ever dying. Not that she found it."

"Oh come on, this is ridiculous. It's one thing to do all this medium business, but you can't expect me to believe fairy tales about living forever."

Suzy frowned. "You have no idea, do you? You haven't got a clue what she was into towards the end, the stuff she was playing with. She had you completely fooled didn't she? Wrapped around her little finger, like most of the men she met. You know that was all an act don't you? You weren't anyone special. You are aware of what happened to her in the end aren't you, when it all went wrong? You do know how she died?"

"I saw it!"

Shit! Jimmy couldn't believe he just blurted that out. Suzy had been goading him, he was still vulnerable from opening up to her about Jennie and he'd reacted without thinking. Suzy's expression changed to shocked indignation.

"What did you just say?" she demanded.

"Nothing."

"It wasn't nothing. You said you saw my sister die.

I knew you were holding something back but I never . . . How did you see her die? Were you there?"

"No, it was nothing like that."

"Is this some kind of twisted game? Have you come round to gloat over what you did? Do you get an extra thrill from torturing the family?"

"No, no, I wasn't there, I wasn't there, alright. It's not like that. I saw a video."

"You saw a video? You mean you get off on this stuff?"

"No, of course not. I didn't want to watch it, I was forced to."

"Forced to?"

"I owed somebody some money okay, one of these hardcore people you were talking about. He sat me down and forced me to watch it, me and a friend. He said he'd do the same to us if he didn't get his money."

"So you haven't actually met Melissa then?"

"Yes, I told you, at the audition later."

"But what does all this have to do with a film of her death?"

"Well, we . . . erm, we sort of got hold of the footage, we were going to use bits of it in the film. Then your sister turned up at the audition and we thought she was a dead ringer for the girl in the footage. We didn't know anything about it. We just thought we'd got lucky, that's all."

"You were going to take footage of my sister's murder and turn it into entertainment?"

"No, of course we weren't, well . . . maybe we were, but it wasn't going to be y'know—tacky or anything."

"Oh really, so how was it going to be?"

"You know, edgy, exciting, hardcore. It's not like anyone she knew was going to see it."

"What if I'd seen it, or another member of my family? How do you think we'd have felt?"

"Why would you see it? Are you into Indie Horror?"

"Does that matter?"

Jimmy dropped his head and stared at the rug beneath his feet, filled with worse self-loathing than he'd felt over Jennie. "No, I guess it doesn't."

Suzy let out a fierce sigh and held up her hands in barely suppressed anger. "This is worse than if you'd murdered her you know? Parading her death in front of total strangers like some sick sideshow. What kind of person are you?"

"Look it's not like that, she's probably not even the girl in the film? She just looks like her. How do you know she's dead? I mean I've met her, spoken with her, maybe she just disappeared for a while, to get away from these people you mentioned, and now she's back."

"She's dead, Jimmy."

"How do you know that?"

"How did I know you were lying? How did I know about Jennie? I have my ways, I find things out and I know she's still in torment."

"Then how come I've seen her? Not just me, but my associate. How is that possible?"

"Did you see her a lot of times when you were in each other's company?"

"No, just twice."

"So she never appeared to you when you were together again?"

"She had all these strange demands about how she wanted to work. She only wanted one other person in the studio with her."

"And did you ever capture her image on film?"

"Yes, well no actually. She turned up for the first day of shooting but there was something up with the camera. She came out all blurry or something. I'm not entirely sure. I didn't see it, my colleague told me about it."

"Did anyone get injured or killed while you were working on the film?"

"No, no one."

"No unexplained deaths?"

"No, well . . . sort of. The guys who forced us to watch the footage. Someone killed them all, while we were watching it, tore them apart, but I didn't see what happened to them."

Jimmy got to his feet and began to pace the small room. He put his hands up to his temples as a wave of panic broke over him. "Shit, it's all so completely fucked up isn't it? I've never said it out loud, the things that happened, but now, just hearing myself talk about it, it's completely fucked up. What's going on. Do you know?"

"I think my sister's spirit is trapped inside that footage."

"Like a possession you mean?"

"Yes, I think this Isimud did it to her, like a kind of sick joke. You spoke about actors living on after they're dead because their image is caught on camera. That's a kind of immortality. I think Isimud captured her spirit at the point of death so she'd live forever in that film."

"How does that involve me?"

'I think you're a lot alike."

"Me and Melissa, you're joking right?"

"No, you both hang on to your pain. Melissa could never let go of it. We didn't have a happy childhood, our father was violent and abusive. Melissa never got over it. It's why she was drawn to the worst kind of men. In her own way, I think she was trying to get back at our father, to overcome what he did to us. It's probably what Isimud used to trap her spirit. It's the one thing people find hardest when they're recovering from a traumatic experience. They feel too guilty to let go of their pain and they torture themselves."

"That's not like me at all."

"Yes it is, look how you reacted to Jennie's death. You've never gotten over it, you haven't allowed yourself. You can't let go of the pain."

Jimmy sighed and heard his chest rattle. He ran his fingers through his hair. "You're right, I haven't gotten over it yet. I don't think I want to. So, you think there's some connection between Melissa and me, is that why I can see her?"

"When you watched the footage you became emotionally involved with her and she was able to manifest herself to you."

"But how could I see her so clearly?"

"Because you wanted to. You invested your own desires and imaginations in her and gave her more substance. Why do you think she asked you to help her and not your colleague, because you still want to help Jennie and you can't."

"But how is that possible, how can a ghost possess a piece of film?"

"A spirit can inhabit, or become trapped, by anything that bears its image while it was alive. Spare, the artist you asked me about, described his paintings as portals and mirrors for the spirit. A film is no different. It preserves the image of a person, as they were when they were alive, how they looked, moved and talked. It's easy for their spirit to become trapped by those moving images, especially if there's trauma involved, like a murder. Melissa's spirit is imprisoned in the footage, like a victim who can't escape the memory of an event. She's forced to relive her murder over and over every time the film is played. That's why she's manifesting, why people are getting hurt. She's desperate and she needs to escape."

"What can we do?"

"You've got to forget this ridiculous film for a start. Bring the footage to me so I can have it exorcised and we can release Melissa's spirit. Then we have to hand all the copies you have over to the police so my sister's killers can be brought to justice."

"The police, are you sure?"

"I'll keep your name out of it, if that's what you're worried about. But you do want to help my sister, don't you? That's what you came here for wasn't it?"

"I guess."

"Then you have to get me that footage."

Jimmy wasn't sure. Suzy seemed convinced about the right thing to do, but he didn't want to get the police involved. Even if she did keep his name out of it they might find something that could drop him right in it.

Before he could say anything, Suzy's eyes rolled up into her sockets and she fell backwards onto the floor.

Jimmy froze, uncertain if this was part of some act. When she didn't move he knelt next to her to see what was wrong. Maybe she'd had a heart attack or something.

Jimmy patted her cheek lightly. "Err, listen, are you alright?" he said. When she didn't respond he checked her pulse and was pleased to find she had one. He put his ear to her mouth to see if she was breathing okay and she jerked, like her muscles were going into a spasm.

Jimmy leapt to his feet, his heart thumping with the shock. Maybe she was having an epileptic fit. Should he try and stop her swallowing her tongue? When he was younger, he'd seen a school nurse shove a wooden spoon into a boy's mouth to stop him swallowing his tongue while he was having a fit. Jimmy wondered if he should check Suzy's kitchen for wooden spoons.

Suzy started to cough, her chest rose and fell with deep, ragged breaths, then she sat up. Only it wasn't Suzy who sat up. She wasn't moving or acting like she had before, it was as though she was someone else entirely.

"Thank God she's gone, the sanctimonious bitch," she said. "She's always been like that, no sense of humour, full of self-importance."

"Suzy, are you . . . are you alright?"

"No, I'm not, and I'm not Suzy either."

"I don't . . . what do you mean?"

"Oh come on lover, don't you recognise me? Okay, I wouldn't have picked this outfit, given the choice, but then I didn't have a choice."

There was something about her voice, it was Suzy's

voice but the nuances were different, so were her mannerisms.

"Wait . . . Melissa?" said Jimmy.

"Oh, so you do remember me. I was beginning to feel a little neglected." She patted the cushion next to her, in a coquettish manner. "Why don't you come and sit next to me."

Jimmy sat on the cushion. She put her hand on his lap and leaned suggestively close. Jimmy could smell the bitter tea on her breath, the oils of her hair and the sweat of her armpits. He pulled away without thinking. She pulled a face.

"Oh, I see," she said. "You don't fancy me when I'm wearing Suzy, and I thought you'd see beyond the flesh, to the real me." She sniffed her armpit. "I don't blame you I suppose, she could do with a bath and a make-over."

"Melissa . . . how are you . . . what are you . . . "

"Doing here? I wanted to see you. This was the quickest and easiest way to get to you. Poor old Suzy's wide open to this sort of thing."

"She says you're trapped inside the footage."

"I am . . . sort of . . . but not in the way she thinks." Her mood changed quite suddenly. She seemed worried and furtive. She reached out for Jimmy and grabbed his arm. "You're still going to come for me aren't you? You won't let me down?"

She turned away from him, her hand to her mouth. "I know I've no right to ask this of you, but you're the only hope I have."

The words cut right through Jimmy. "Of course I'm going to come for you," he said. "Do you want me to get the footage to Suzy?"

"No," she said, with sudden alarm. "For Christ's sake don't do that, anything but that. I can't have her interfering with this. You promised to be my Dumuzi, remember?"

"Of course?"

"Well that's what I need from you, come to Hell for me."

"Hell?" Jimmy sounded alarmed.

Melissa made Suzy pout. "You promised. I need you. You said you'd come back for me."

Jimmy put his hands to his temples. He was having a hard time with the emotional guilt. "Okay, but what do I have to do?"

"You need to find Mr Isimud."

"And how do I do that?"

"Take the footage to the Tailor of the True Cloth."

"Who?"

"Ask around, he's hard to find but it's not beyond you. Take the footage to him, everything else will become clear."

"I'm really not following you, you're not making a lot of sense . . . "

"Quick, you have to go now, Suzy's fighting me and I can't hold her down much longer. She's stronger than she looks. Go now, right now, before she comes back."

She slumped to the ground and began to stir and thrash as though she were waking from a bad dream. Jimmy stood and let himself out the front door.

CHAPTER TWENTY

THE FOOTAGE ENDED and the screen went blank. Sam got carefully up from the sofa, so as not to hurt his cock. It was so chafed and raw it hurt to even look at, let alone touch.

He couldn't decide whether to re-watch the footage, or grab a beer and some left over pizza. He hadn't had anything to eat or drink in over eight hours. He looked around the room at the chipped paint on the floorboards, the mouldering furniture and the curtainless windows. There wasn't any pizza left. The discarded box was empty and so were the beer cans scattered at his feet.

His stomach rumbled in complaint. He was hungry, but he'd run out of provisions. He could order another pizza but that would mean going downstairs to the pub; the delivery guy wasn't allowed up to the room. Going downstairs meant he'd have to interact with the people in the bar. It also meant putting pants on, and he wasn't sure his poor cock could take that.

Maybe it was best if he just stayed in his room and watched the footage one more time. He'd rented the room, above the pub in Chalk Farm, so he wouldn't be disturbed. So he would be left alone and it would be just him and the footage. He needed a place where he could watch it as many times as he needed.

Sam had lost count of the times he'd seen it now. It was just about all he'd been doing since that night when Melissa . . . when she . . . Sam couldn't continue the thought. The memory of what happened was too raw for him to process, but it wouldn't leave him alone. It haunted him relentlessly, crowding out every other thought from his mind. The only thing that kept the memories at bay was watching the footage.

The minute the footage stopped, the events of that night came flooding back. He still didn't understand what had happened. He kept wanting to believe it was an hallucination caused by post-traumatic stress. That the events in the lock up had hit him harder than he realised, and he was seeing things.

No matter how hard he tried to believe this, he knew it wasn't true. He had no idea how Melissa had done the things she'd done, or why she'd wanted to do them to him. Sam felt, on some instinctive level, that he was being punished for what he'd planned to do with the footage. No-one deserved to be punished like that though, no matter what they'd done.

She just hadn't stopped. No matter how many times he'd said: "no." He wasn't sure when he stopped saying it aloud, but he kept on saying it in his head, right up until the end.

Wounds had kept opening up in her flesh. Every time something happened to the woman in the footage, Melissa's body would spontaneously develop the same injury. Then she'd find some way to force Sam to penetrate it. Her blood coating his swollen member, layers of fat and muscle parting to welcome him inside. She gripped him with her sinews, tissues and stomach wall, refusing to let him soften till she was done with him.

Sam had fought the urge to come, dragging himself back from the brink of orgasm, hardly able to believe he could get aroused by what Melissa was doing to him. It was as if his body was betraying him, giving Melissa its tacit approval by getting so turned on. Just when he thought he'd mastered himself she would do something else to him and there would be another surge towards climax.

Sam ended up hating his physical self, not just for being so turned on, but for turning on him. When the sight of Melissa's torn and ragged flesh got too much for him, Sam closed his eyes. This didn't stop Melissa. Every noise the woman in the footage made, Melissa made simultaneously, as though they were a chorus of backing singers, wailing in pain.

Finally she fell off him and hit the ground with a sickening crunch. Sam could tell by the sounds of the footage that the blurred figures had moved on to the third man. He didn't open his eyes to see what sort of state Melissa was in.

Sam just listened as the flayed and ruptured remains of Melissa crawled towards the door. He didn't want to see what sort of shape she'd become, and that made it worse, never knowing quite what state his violator had been in at the end. His mind tortured him far more with the images it conjured from the wet, ruined sounds of her sliding across the floor.

The footage finally stopped and he waited a few minutes before opening his eyes. The studio was silent.

There was a trail of smeared blood from the chair to the door. Even in the waning light he could see it was already fading.

Sam had pulled up his jeans and grabbed his coat. He shut the laptop and picked it up. For a moment he considered dashing it to the floor and destroying it, destroying every copy of the footage, but something stopped him. He wasn't sure what.

He followed Melissa's trail of blood as he left the studio, walked along the corridor and then down the stairs. It became less and less evident with every flight of steps and by the time he reached the door it had disappeared. Sam knew that by morning there would be no trace of it anywhere in the building.

CHAPTER TWENTY-ONE

WHEN HE'D GOTTEN back to his apartment, even though it was late, the first thing Sam did was get straight in the shower.

In a repeat of the night he got back from the lock up, Sam stood beneath the scalding hot water and tried to wash away the memories of the previous hours. He was no more successful this time than he had been the last. No amount of soap or water could wash away the spectre of Melissa's touch. He could still feel her ragged skin pressing against his, her breath on his cheek and her blood spilling out over his loins. Every time he closed his eyes he saw her face and the gaping hole in her throat.

His skin was red and smarting when he left the shower. The images in his mind were just as vivid. They weren't the only thing he couldn't escape. His whole body was filled with an invisible pressure, an insatiable need for release. He'd fought off his desire to come with Melissa and now it dogged him mercilessly.

Sam was reminded of a Sunday afternoon he'd spent, many years ago, with Amanda, his first serious girlfriend. She went to the sister school of his boarding school. They'd met at one of the crummy balls their schools set up and had actually hit it off.

Amanda was a day girl, so her parents lived in the area. Sam was allowed a free weekend every third week. Instead of hanging out with the other deadbeats, whose parents couldn't be bothered collecting them, Sam would visit Amanda's house.

He was allowed to stay in the annexe, where her Gran used to live before her coronary. He and Amanda had to be extremely careful sneaking into each other's rooms because Amanda's parents were like hawks, but otherwise Sam was always made to feel very welcome.

On this particular afternoon, Sam was lying on the patchwork quilt Amanda's great grandmother made, with his trousers round his ankles, while Amanda gave him head. She was getting pretty good at it, too. Amanda had only had one other lover and Sam was a virgin before they met, so they pretty much learned everything together.

Amanda had just looked up, while he was still in her mouth, and caught Sam's eye. She made a little 'uh-huh' noise to signal that it was okay to come in her mouth for the first time. Sam, who had been on the verge of letting go, hardly had time to get excited about this when they heard Amanda's mother coming down the short corridor that connected the annexe to the main house. Amanda leapt up while Sam yanked his trousers back on, getting his boxers all twisted. Amanda's mum had popped her head round the door to tell them that lunch was on the table.

Sam only noticed his fly was still down when he sat down at the table. Unfortunately, he probably wasn't the only one who noticed, because Amanda's dad called him away to watch the rugby on Sky Sport the minute the meal was over, and Amanda's mum had

Amanda come and help with the dishes. In fact her parents made sure they didn't spend a moment alone together until it was time for Amanda's dad to drop Sam back at school.

When Sam arrived, his housemaster called him in to his study and told him he'd be sharing his room with a Norwegian pupil, who'd just this minute arrived. He would have to share with Sam until space could be found to house the poor chap. Sam fell asleep that night to the sound of the Norwegian droning on about his cross country skiing trophies.

Sam's dick had remained hard the entire time and the only thing he could think about was Amanda looking up at him and going "uh-huh." Everything else that happened from that point on was just background noise. That one image and his desperate need for release drowned everything else out. The torment it caused was unbearable. Sam had never wanted to come so badly in his life and he hadn't been able to.

That entire experience was nothing compared to what he felt when Melissa was finished with him. Every nerve ending in his flesh, every molecule of his body, was screaming with the need to ejaculate. The compulsion was like a rabid dog that had its fangs in his soul. He was haunted by the ghost of the orgasm he hadn't had.

Sam spent nearly two hours trying to fight the urge, but it was a losing battle. His mind was under siege from the mental images and his body was wracked by the need for release. He had to do something to alleviate the pressure, to bring some release from the mental anguish.

He glanced at the laptop on the coffee table, and he

knew the only thing that would quiet the torment he was in. He opened the laptop, pulled out his cock and clicked on the footage. He used gentle strokes to keep himself hard throughout the first death, saving himself for Melissa's appearance. It was definitely Melissa in the footage. The whole experience had made him sure of that.

When she appeared on the screen Sam throbbed so hard he had to let go of himself for fear of shooting straight away. He wanted to draw this out, to savour every moment. He was so backed up he was going to need a huge build up to get it all out of his system.

The first orgasm, when it came, just at the point where Melissa expired, was so intense Sam strained his jaw from screaming. When he was done, the scream became a sob. A deep well of self-hatred rose up within him. He watched the final scenes of the footage with a dull-eyed gaze of despair.

When it finished, Sam took hold of his cock, clicked back to the beginning and started the footage all over again. That first orgasm, big as it was, hadn't cleared away everything, hadn't even begun to scratch the surface in fact. If anything, it only increased the pressure building within him, as though he was trying to release something that was too large for his body to contain.

The second orgasm did nothing to alleviate this, it only stoked the insistent urge. The need was so deep within Sam that he feared some poisonous desire had infected his soul and this was the only way to lance it.

Sam played the footage and brought himself off time and again until he collapsed from exhaustion and slept fitfully. When he woke, some hours later, he started all over again, but no amount of self-abuse could rid him of the phantom orgasm that refused to come. It had its claws sunk deep in the core of his being and the more he tried to discharge it, the more it clung on and tortured him.

At the end of the second day, Sam realised he wasn't going to be able to dodge his mobile, his e-mail or the doorbell forever. Sooner or later someone was going to get in and get hold of him. He wasn't about to let that happen.

He found a room on a local letting agency site, gathered up a few clothes, a couple of bags of provisions, and grabbed the laptop with the footage on it. Before he left, Sam made a point of destroying every back up copy of the footage. He was like a jealous lover, guarding the fidelity of his partner, ensuring no one could have her but him.

CHAPTER TWENTY-TWO

SAM HAD BEEN in the room above the pub ever since. Though he'd watched the footage more times than he could remember, he'd never seen the exact same sequence twice. The footage changed every time he watched it. That's why he'd never been able to edit it.

To begin with the changes were quite subtle, but in time everything was different from the first time he saw it. At first Sam noticed how the blurry, shadow figures altered the way they tortured the three victims. They seemed to get crueller, more extreme and increasingly creative in the ways they flayed and dismembered them.

After this, the victims began to change, the two men he'd originally seen with Melissa were replaced with others, including the men who'd been in the lock up with Ashkan. The only constant throughout the whole of Sam's viewing was the presence of Melissa. That and the almost transcendent way she bore the torture of the blurred figures.

In time Sam began to suspect that the footage itself had a basic consciousness, one that was devious and malign. He knew it was aware of him watching, that's why it kept changing things. It was testing him, probing him, trying to discover the limits of what he could endure as an observer so it could push him beyond it.

That's why it had killed Ashkan and his crew, torn their bodies apart and taken them into itself, where they could be tortured endlessly every time the footage was played. Ashkan and his men had weakened. They had given in to the horror of what the footage was showing them and they failed the test. They weren't desensitised enough to the violence and atrocities.

Sam knew the only thing keeping him alive was the phantom orgasm that still plagued his being. That held him rapt, in front of the laptop, watching repeatedly, working his raw cock ragged until he was practically blowing air when he came.

No matter how inured he was to what he was viewing, no matter how many layers of mental and emotional protection he put up against the horror of it, Sam had always known it was only a matter of time before the footage went too far, found the one thing he couldn't stomach and claimed him. That had now become his main reason for watching.

Some small part of his psyche, some tiny part of his consciousness screaming away at the back of his mind, was demanding an end to what Sam was doing, to what he had become. And there was only one way to end it. The imminent fear of total destruction, of being claimed by the one thing he feared most, was the aphrodisiac Sam needed. It was the fuel he craved to ignite that last monster of an orgasm, the one that had claimed his soul and now needed to be exorcised from his being.

Sam reached into the tub of Nivea Creme on the

arm of the sofa and grabbed a fistful, coating his palm liberally. In spite of the cream, the cracked and peeling skin of his cock stung viciously as he took hold of it. He started up the footage.

Sam noted the most recent changes with a dispassionate curiosity. It was a way of distancing himself from the footage, so it wouldn't get to him. Sometimes the changes were so minor you couldn't spot them, other times they were so profound Sam did a double take.

Whatever the changes, Sam never failed to get hard by the time Melissa came on the screen. The mixture of longing and violation she stirred in him always swelled him, no matter how sore he was.

The figures went through the same rituals of torture and dismemberment as they had the previous few times. If there were any deviations they were so minor Sam missed them. Until the camera pushed in for a close up he hadn't seen before.

It focused on Melissa's face looking directly out at him. From her expression and the way her eyes met his, he could tell she knew he was watching. The camera pushed in closer and Melissa mouthed two words. The shot wasn't fully in focus, so Sam didn't catch what she said. He narrowed his eyes in concentration and she mouthed it again. Two words:

'Forgive me.'

And this was finally too much for Sam.

That Melissa, in the midst of her torment and degradation, would beg his forgiveness was too much for him to bear. It made him realise the extent of what she'd done to him. What she'd taken away and what she'd turned him into. More importantly, Sam realised that what was going to happen to him, was worse than Melissa was suffering.

A giant gob of white cream dripped from Sam's finger as he reached over to his laptop to shut the footage off, to call 'uncle' and admit he'd had enough. The movement was involuntary but, even as he made it, Sam knew it was a mistake.

The laptop screen seemed to bulge and flare with brightness. The room was filled with a light so fierce Sam had to shield his eyes. The image on the screen started to grow, and as it got larger the borders of the picture started to fray, as though little tendrils of light were spilling from the edges, trying to find purchase in the room.

Sam got the awful sense that the barriers between the reality inside the screen and the reality all around him were breaking down, like a small pool of water joining a larger one. There appeared to be a run-off from the edges of the screen into his room.

At the very periphery of his vision he saw three blurred and shadowy figures pour out of the corners of the screen. It wasn't the same three figures in the footage, but three further blurry creatures who seemed to have been waiting just off camera. Sam couldn't look at any of them directly, but he knew they were there, circling him, until, with a sudden swiftness, they struck.

Sam winced as one of the figures took hold of his cock and began to stroke it with expert fingers. The figure's touch brought a tingle to his skin, like a light electrical discharge. Another of the figures slipped its hands under his T-shirt and tugged it up until Sam's chest was bare. The figure took hold of Sam's nipples and squeezed hard, making him yelp.

Sam knew that he ought to be fighting the figures, attempting to break their grip on him and get out of the room. He just couldn't conceive of any way to do that. He was frozen in place and powerless to stop them.

The third figure removed his trousers, cupped his buttocks and pulled them gently apart. It pushed first one, then two fingers up his rectum. With a stab of pain, that was almost exciting, the fingers found his prostate gland and began to massage it.

The pain from the figures' ministrations grew to such an intensity it was as if they knew how to find nerve endings no physician or anatomist had ever identified. Yet the agony was more stimulating and more thrilling than any sensation Sam had ever known.

There was no viciousness or spite in the figures' touch. For all the torment they were causing, their attentions seemed to contain a certain sorrowful kindness, like surgeons weeping over an un-anaesthetised patient.

Even still, the levels of agony Sam was experiencing continued to rise. As the figures' hands seemed to meld with his damaged flesh Sam hit a blinding wall of pain with such velocity that he broke right through it. Something inside him broke, too—it was the part of him that had been holding back that phantom orgasm.

The floodgates had been blown wide open. Sam felt the orgasm he'd been desperate to get out of his system, come towards him from a million miles away, at what felt like the speed of light. When it hit, it was like an internal implosion. His balls retreated up into his body and then kept on going. He felt tubes tear and veins snap as his testicles were drawn right up inside him.

The force of the orgasm was like a black hole within him, tearing every internal organ towards his cock. Sam felt his bladder collapse with a searing wrench and his lower colon follow it.

He watched with awe as an impossibly large bulge appeared at the base of his cock, then travelled its length until the helmet swelled up, his urethra was torn open and a torrent of blood and decimated body tissue shot from the end of his cock.

Sam screamed with pain and terror, and an impossible ecstasy, as thick, red streams of viscera spurted out of him. He saw his stomach wall fold in on itself as his small intestines were ripped out of him and ejaculated into the slick pool of gore that was soaking the grimy rug at his feet.

The screen in front of him grew larger until it filled his vision with a fierce glow. He remembered something about dead spirits being encouraged to move towards the light and realised this was the only light he was going to see in his dying moments. Sam knew where he was headed, and he knew what was going to happen to him when he got there. He'd spent days watching and now it was his turn.

He felt the orgasm crush his lungs and shatter his ribcage, then he ceased to feel his body at all. The only sensation left was the orgasm itself, still raging, still clawing at him until all that remained of him was its explosive force.

It lifted him up and conveyed him through the screen into the footage itself.

And that was when his real torment began.

CHAPTER TWENTY-THREE

"YEAH, LIKE I SAID," the barman called over his shoulder, "we ain't seen him in days, mate. Landlord reckons he's done a bunk." He was a bulky man who huffed a lot as he led Jimmy up the stairs. He was losing most of his hair, even though he was only in his late twenties, and had grown a huge pair of mutton chop whiskers to compensate.

"Landlord's coming back this evening to clear the room, so if you want anything you best go through his stuff and grab it now, alright? Good luck though, it's minging in there."

"That's okay, I'm only after one thing, I shan't be long."

The barman coughed, looked at the floor and scratched his neck, waiting for something.

"Oh yeah, sorry," said Jimmy and pulled two twenties and a ten from his pocket.

"Cheers," said the barman, taking the money. He produced a key, unlocked the door then turned and lumbered back down the stairs.

The smell hit Jimmy the minute he opened the door. The air was stale and stank of Sam's unwashed body. There was also another stench, underneath the BO, a coppery, sweet metallic scent, that Jimmy'd smelled once before.

It had taken Jimmy a while to track Sam down. When he hadn't been able to reach him by conventional means, Jimmy had let himself into Sam's apartment with the spare key. He'd scoured the place but found no trace of the footage. Sam had left loads of equipment behind, including two laptops and his iMac, but none of them had any files containing the footage.

Sam appeared, at first, to have disappeared without a trace. Most of his clothes were still in his closet. There was food in the fridge and his horror film and memorabilia collection was still on its shelves. This worried Jimmy so he did some digging.

Jimmy fired up the iMac and, after a few guesses at Sam's password, got into his e-mail. A bit of digging through the different folders led Jimmy to an e-mail from a letting agent where he found Sam had rented a room above some pub, just up the road in Chalk Farm.

Jimmy had no idea why Sam wanted to do that, but he figured it was his best lead. Maybe someone was threatening Sam and he'd gone to ground. Chances are, if they were threatening Sam they'd be after Jimmy next. It could be one of Ashkan's associates, perhaps they'd finally made the connection with his disappearance.

It might even be this Mr Isimud character that Melissa and Suzy spoke about. If Isimud was looking for them Jimmy might not have to go looking for this tailor chap, so long as he could track down the footage. Whatever the case he needed to get hold of Sam.

At first glance the room seemed like a dead end. There was an old sofa and some rickety chairs in the space, that was it. Looking round Jimmy saw some of

Sam's clothes scattered among the empty take away boxes and beer cans. That in itself was kind of weird. Sam was usually meticulous about his clothes and any place he stayed was always spotless.

Jimmy approached the sofa, his heart beat faster when he saw the laptop sitting on an old wooden stool. He walked round the sofa and tapped the keyboard. It was almost out of charge but the screen came up and showed him what might be the last remaining copy of the footage. It was only after he'd silently punched the air that Jimmy noticed the huge puddle of blood and shredded body tissue seeping into the rug under the stool.

Jimmy knew instantly who the puddle had once been. That horrific realisation drained all the life and energy out of him. His limbs lost all their strength and he crashed to the sofa. His stomach turned over and he leaned forward just in time to empty it.

When he'd finished retching, Jimmy sat back and wiped his mouth. He forced himself to glance over at the puddle and noted, almost peripherally, that it was smaller than when he'd last looked. He took a proper look and saw that the puddle was shrinking incrementally, just like the puddles of Ashkan and his men. Jimmy knew by the time the Landlord dropped in that evening there would be nothing left but a spot on the rug. Although his puke would be drying nicely.

Whatever had happened to Ashkan and his crew had now happened to Sam. It was connected in some way to watching the footage, but Jimmy had no idea how. He also had no idea why Sam had rented a shithole like this one to work on the footage when they were still paying rent on the studio space.

Not to mention all the kit Sam had back at his apartment.

Maybe he was trying a different environment for inspiration, or just needed some space or something, but it didn't make much sense. Then again, nothing in Jimmy's life made any sense since he'd been forced to watch the footage.

The only person he might have spoken to about it, the only person who might have understood, was Sam. It seemed like Sam was the only real friend Jimmy had left, and now he was gone, chewed up and spat out by whatever crazy shit they'd gotten themselves into.

Jimmy lay back on the sofa and stared up at the ceiling. The loss of Sam, and the sudden grief this brought, was like a boulder on his chest, crushing all the breath out of him. Jimmy had gotten his friend into this. He was responsible for Sam's death. If only he hadn't been chasing after some spirit trapped in a piece of film, maybe he'd have been able to help Sam.

The regret was like an old, old friend. He'd been here before. It was exactly how he felt when Jennie died. Jimmy squeezed his eyes shut and tried to find one slender thread of consolation in the black mood that was closing in on him.

He needed a lifeline, or he was going to go under fast. That's what had happened the previous time. He scrabbled around for some tiny consolation to cling to, something to keep him afloat. Maybe this wasn't like the previous times. It's just possible that things were different. He'd promised Melissa he'd come for her, just like he'd promised Jennie, but this time he was coming.

He'd wasted his time trying to save Benny, but he

hadn't made that mistake with Sam, who was probably just as doomed. There was still a chance to redeem himself, to make all this right and make up for the mistake he made with Jennie. If only he could reach Melissa and rescue her from the film she was trapped in.

Jimmy opened his eyes and took a deep breath, it was like breaking the surface of the ocean after he'd been heading down to its floor. He knew what those black moods could do to him and he'd just about staved this one off. He hadn't even needed a line of coke. He might just have bought himself a reprieve.

He just needed to keep active, stay focused and remain one step ahead of the black dog, otherwise that bastard would be on him before he could blink. Jimmy got to his feet, found one of Sam's shirts on the sofa and dropped it over the pool of puke to cover it up. Then he grabbed the laptop and left the room without a backward glance at the puddle that had once been his friend.

Downstairs in the pub, the barman was busy with a couple of punters. Jimmy slipped out of the door with the laptop under his arm, glad not to have caught his eye.

CHAPTER TWENTY-FOUR

JIMMY LET HIMSELF into Sam's apartment and put the laptop on the coffee table in the living room. The presence of the laptop in the apartment seemed to confirm Sam's absence. He was never coming back. Like Jennie he was dead and lost to Jimmy forever.

Jimmy sat on the sofa and stared at the laptop as though it was booby trapped. In a way it was. It contained the last surviving copy of the footage. Someone, or something, connected with that footage had killed Sam. Jimmy was afraid to even open the laptop, let alone switch it on.

He knew the footage was dangerous, toxic on some level he could barely comprehend. Everyone who'd watched the footage, since Ashkan first played it in the lock up, was dead. Everyone except Jimmy. Was it simply a matter of time before it claimed him, too?

The wise thing to do would be to destroy the footage, but it was more important to his plans than it had ever been. Using it in a film had been all about redeeming the terrible situation in which he first saw it. Now he wanted to use it to redeem himself.

Too many people knew of its existence to use the footage in a film. He'd moved on from that. He needed the footage to save Melissa. That was his next big project.

In many ways it was an obvious development from the film, especially given its subject matter. The story was spilling over into the real world. He was searching for the girl in the cellar, just like DC Harlow, taking the role of Dumuzi to Melissa's Inanna. It was art becoming life.

Jimmy had wanted one good thing to come out of his experience in the lock up. Something he could hang on to. This was it. He could do something good. Melissa needed his help. The footage was the key to that. He just needed to learn how to turn that key and unlock what was going on.

That's what Sam would have wanted. Sam had fought to keep this movie going, even when Jimmy had changed tack and gone off looking for Melissa. If he was still alive now, he would be fighting to keep the movie alive.

The best way to honour Sam's memory, and make something good come from his death, was to continue the project in its new direction. Doing something truly positive with the footage. Not exploiting the victims in the footage, but saving one of them.

Jimmy still didn't understand everything that was going on. He knew Melissa was trapped in some way in the footage. Living through her death over and over again. She could obviously break out for short periods, though he didn't know how.

Maybe she knew that Jimmy was watching her that time in the lock up. She'd seen Jimmy close his eyes, and knew he was different from the others watching her. So she reached out to him for assistance.

She knew he wouldn't have believed her if she'd told him what was really happening straight away, so she'd played along with the film idea until she could enlist his help. She needed him to find this mysterious Mr Isimud. Jimmy imagined he was the type of man who didn't want to be found, and took steps to ensure that. This other guy she'd mentioned, the Tailor of the True Cloth, was probably the same.

It would take a certain amount of resources to find those kinds of people. Resources Jimmy didn't have. But Sam might have them.

Jimmy left the sofa and went to the desk in Sam's bedroom. That's where he kept his personal laptop. Jimmy booted it up and was delighted to discover Sam's internet browser had saved all his passwords. This made it even easier to get into Sam's bank account, especially once Jimmy found the file containing all his security details.

Upon close inspection, it appeared Sam did have enough money in his savings and current account to fund Jimmy's project. At some point however, he might have to sell Sam's apartment, if he needed bigger funds. It was worth quite a bit due to its location.

Jimmy had a pang of conscience as he transferred the majority of the money to his own account. He assured himself that Sam would have used the money to finish the film anyway. As finding Melissa was just an extension of the film, a new development in an ongoing project, then Sam was in effect still funding the film, and Jimmy was putting his money to use in a way Sam would have approved.

The only thing to worry about was someone close

to Sam noticing his disappearance and investigating his bank transactions. Jimmy thought he was fairly safe there. Sam hadn't been in contact with his parents for a while and all his other friends were close to Jimmy, too.

No one could prove that Sam hadn't moved the money himself. They were always transferring money between each other's accounts. Jimmy could never be accused of any wrong doing regarding Sam's disappearance. Not only did he have an alibi, but there was no body and no physical trace left of Sam whatsoever.

Sam would have wanted this project to be seen through to the end, he was a diehard. Jimmy was doing this for Sam, every bit as much as Melissa, now. He had the funds and the footage. Tomorrow he would start spreading some money around to see if he couldn't get a lead on this Tailor guy.

CHAPTER TWENTY-FIVE

ARE YOU SURE you've got the right spot?" Jimmy said, glancing at his watch.

"Yeah," said Rick, a tall, bulky guy with close cropped ginger hair. He stubbed out his cigarette and put his hands in the pockets of his grey hoodie. "He always makes you wait, he's worse than a dealer that way."

They were standing on a dark corner in the back streets of Shoreditch. Rick glanced up and down the road then lit another cigarette.

Jimmy had met Rick through Alfie. Quite predictably, Alfie had taken the piss the minute Jimmy asked him if he knew anyone who was into hardcore magic, the really dangerous stuff? When he'd had his fun, Alfie introduced Jimmy to Rick. Jimmy explained to Rick that he was looking for someone called 'the Tailor of the True Cloth.'

"I think you'll need Vince for that," Rick had said. "Have you heard of him?"

Jimmy shook his head. "No."

"Some people call him the 'Mystic Yardie,' but never to his face. Other people call him 'The Baron,' after Baron Samedi, the Loa he serves."

"The 'what' he serves?"

Rick scowled. "Don't you know nothing about this stuff?"

"Not really no, I'm afraid. This is all new to me."

"Followers of voodoo call themselves 'Servants of the Loa.' The Loa are the invisible entities they worship. Every follower has a like a patron Loa, a Met Tet they call it. Vince's Met Tet is Baron Samedi, a Loa of the dead. If he likes you, he'll let you call him Vince."

"How will I know if he likes me?"

"You'll know if he doesn't like you. Seriously, this is one dangerous bastard you're dealing with. He's done literally hundreds of hits for different east end gangs. No one ever finds the bodies, it's like they never existed when he's done. That's why he's always in demand."

Jimmy thought of the bodies he'd seen disappear and shuddered. "So he knows his stuff, when it comes to the dark arts, then?"

"He practices Petro-Voodoun."

"Sounds like an 80s synth band."

"You see, it's comments like that, that could get you killed."

"I'm sorry, tell me about this Petrol Voodoo."

"That's Petro-Voodoun, there are different schools of voodoo see, different paths you can follow as a believer, and each one has its own rites and rituals. Petro-Voodoun is the path you follow if you want to do all the dangerous stuff, and get the really big guns to help you."

"The big guns?"

"The really powerful Loa. Look man, if you don't know any of this shit, why are you spreading all this money around looking for a man like the Tailor?"

Jimmy looked at his watch again. "It's kinda personal, I don't really want to go into it. Does it matter that much, so long as I'm paying you?"

"I guess not." Rick finished his cigarette and lit another one. There was a a tidy little pile of dog ends at his feet. Jimmy realised that for all his front, Rick was pretty nervous about seeing Vince. He wondered if he should be nervous, then decided he didn't care so long as Vince took him to the Tailor.

"So did he learn all this voodoo stuff in Jamaica then?"

Rick scowled and shook his head with disbelief. "No, he's not Jamaican."

"I thought you had to be, to be a yardie."

"You know nothing. And he's not a yardie, he just does hits for the different gangs. He's from Haiti, that's where he learned about voodoo. His mother was a Mambo, a voodoo high priestess, she's like some kind of royalty out there amongst the followers, his whole family is."

Then, as though the mention of Vince's family had conjured him, a beaten up, blue BMW pulled up at the curb. Neither of them had seen or heard it approach. Rick went white, dropped his cigarette and ground it out with his foot.

The back window wound down. Inside the car, Jimmy could see a tall, rangy black guy with shoulder length dreads and a leather jacket.

"So, I hear there's a white boy flashing his cash around trying to find me," said the guy from the backseat. He had a cockney accent, but his voice was deep and surprisingly musical.

"Yeah Vince, this is Jimmy," said Rick. "He's the one who's been asking after you."

Vince didn't say anything to this. He just stared out of the back seat at Rick with a grim expression. Rick coughed and looked down at the floor like a schoolboy who's just been scolded. Vince turned back to Jimmy.

"I need to find the Tailor of the True Cloth," said Jimmy. "I'm told you can help me."

Vince kissed his teeth and said in a perfect Jamaican accent: "Try Saville Row." His window began to close. Jimmy reached out and placed his hand on top of the pane to stop it. Vince bristled. Jimmy suddenly realised how dangerous this was, like putting your hand into a lion's open jaws.

"Look, I'm serious and I can pay," he said. "If you don't know where he is, just let me know and I'll find someone else who does." Jimmy was trying to sound earnest, and hide his desperation. Vince raised an eyebrow at Jimmy's impertinence.

"I know where the Tailor is, and I know what it takes to find him. What I don't know is whether you're up to the job?"

"I'm up to it, and I'm good for the cash. Just tell me what I need to do and I'll do it."

Vince barked out a short humorous laugh. "We'll see about that white boy. Meet me back here on Thursday, same time and bring five grand in cash." Vince looked directly at Rick and said: "Come alone."

Jimmy heard a slight sizzle then felt a searing pain across the palm of his hand. The window was suddenly white hot. He jerked his hand away in agony. The window slowly closed to the sound of Vince's mirthless chuckle.

The blue beamer pulled away from the curb.

Jimmy hugged his hand to his chest as the pain shot up his arm. The car disappeared.

Rick was breathing so heavily he was about to hyperventilate. He pulled out his cigarettes but his hands were shaking too much to light one.

CHAPTER TWENTY-SIX

JIMMY DIDN'T KNOW Peckham well, it was a part of London he'd never been to. In fact, he never really went south of the river Thames. It had taken him all night to find the shebeen.

It was in the basement of an abandoned warehouse, at the bottom of a set of concrete steps that stank of piss. He pushed open the battered steel fire door and peered inside.

He saw nothing, at first, it was so dark. But he could hear muttering voices, the clink of glasses and the scraping of chairs. He wondered if we would find Vince here, or whether this would be another fruitless search.

As his eyes adjusted to the gloom, Jimmy saw a tall, lean figure, with shoulder length dreads, sitting alone with his back to the far wall. Vince didn't see Jimmy as he entered the drinking den, a long thin room with a rubble strewn floor, littered with a collection of near broken furniture. Dim figures sat about makeshift tables and an obese bar man stood behind a ramshackle bar.

Vince looked up as Jimmy approached him and flashed a broad, dangerous smile, showing off his three gold teeth.

"Careful now," said Vince. "White boy like you is like to get shivved in a place like this."

Jimmy found he couldn't control his temper as he sidled up to Vince. "What the fuck happened to you?" he said. "I waited ages and you never showed up."

Vince dropped the smile and sat bolt upright at this. "You gwan disrespeck I white boy? Nuff men die fi less!"

Jimmy held his hands up in apology. Vince was talking in patois, that wasn't a good sign. Jimmy was the only white face in the whole place. He was not in the best position to assert himself.

"Sorry," he said. "I'm not trying to disrespect you. It's just . . . y'know . . . you didn't turn up, and I paid you a lot of money."

Vince stared hard at Jimmy. His eyes bulged and his lips were set. He radiated murderous intent, like a wild beast about to strike. It was hard to endure. Jimmy neither wanted to look away nor at Vince. He was afraid that any reaction might result in a quick and painful death. No-one in the whole shebeen said a word or made a noise.

Just as this became unbearable, Vince threw back his head and let out a deep, throaty laugh, banging the table and pointing at Jimmy. The laughter spread out around the basement, everyone chuckling at Jimmy from the shadows. Jimmy nearly let go of his bladder he was so relieved.

"Sit down blood," Vince said, in a broad east end accent. "Drink some Sammi."

Vince called out to the huge barman in an African language Jimmy didn't recognise. It was some sort of Khosian dialect with lots of tongue clicking, Vince sounded as though he'd been speaking it all his life. It was disconcerting the way a supposedly Haitian guy could switch so effortlessly between so many voices and identities. Jimmy supposed that's why he did it.

"What happened?" said Jimmy. "I gave you the five grand like you asked. I waited on that street corner for hours, freezing my butt off. You pulled up in your beamer and took the money. But the place you told me to meet you at, the next day, doesn't exist. It's taken me days to find you. Why'd you rip me off?"

"I didn't rip you off, you simply passed the first test."

"What do you mean?"

"The knowledge I have, the knowledge you want, does not come cheap and it does not come easily. You have to earn it and you have to prove that you are worthy of it. I am just as hard to find as this knowledge, yet you sought me out. You passed the first test. The next one won't be so simple or so cheap."

"I don't consider five grand to be cheap."

"Then you don't know what my knowledge costs."

The barman arrived with two chipped mugs and an old plastic bottle full of clear liquid. Vince handed Jimmy a mug and poured some of the liquid into it. Jimmy took a sip and started coughing violently. It tasted like marzipan melted in battery acid.

Vince laughed. "You don't like Sammi? You'll never be a rude boy."

"I can live with that."

"So tell me, why do want to find the Tailor?"

Jimmy wasn't sure if he could fully trust Vince, but he figured he didn't have much of a choice, and he might learn something from him. "It's a means to an ends really. I have something I need to take to him and that's supposed to help me get in contact with a guy called Mr Isimud."

Vince inhaled sharply, pursed his lips and shook his head. He looked tense. It was the first time Jimmy had seen him act anything but nonchalant.

"You want to contact Mr Isimud, that's a whole other matter."

"Wait, you know him?"

"He is a man of power. I know everyone with power in this city."

"You mean politicians, fixers, that sort of thing?"

"No, I'm talking about real power, the power to change things forever. I would be very careful if I were you. If you're looking for Mr Isimud, you can guarantee he already knows."

"He knows I'm coming?"

"Oh yes. And it's not likely to end well for you."

"I'll take my chances. So, if you know this Isimud character, could you take me directly to him?"

"No, once he's chosen the route for you to find him, you have to stick to it. I wouldn't go against that."

Jimmy was surprised to see the tiniest glimmer of fear in Vince's eyes when talking about Mr Isimud.

"So there's no other way to find Mr Isimud except through the Tailor?"

"No."

"Can he really make someone immortal?"

"You'd have to ask him. He's certainly been alive for thousands of years."

"Thousands of years, is that possible?"

"So you doubt my words now, white boy?"

"No, no, not at all, I just wondered how that was possible?"

"He conjured up some powerful forces and he created something monstrous, something that's kept him alive ever since."

"Something monstrous?"

"Yes, you're too ignorant to realise, but you've already met it. You carry its scent." Something in the way Vince said this, made Jimmy cold all over.

"Okay," he said. "So let's get back to this Tailor guy. What's his angle? What does his name mean? What exactly is the 'True Cloth?'"

"What do you think it is? There's only one true cloth, the one thing that clothes everything in existence—the fabric of reality. It's what the whole of the universe is cut from and it's the material he chooses to work with."

"Okay, now you've totally lost me. Are you telling me he makes like . . . reality suits?"

Vince sighed. "No, that's not what I'm saying. He offers a unique service to a very select clientele. But first they have to find him."

"That's where you come in."

"Exactly."

"And what is this 'unique service?'"

"He can make a garment out of anything, and I don't just mean any type of fabric. He can fashion dresses from murderous intent and suits from endless longing. He can dress you in the jealous rage of a jilted lover or the bitter lies of a prosecution witness. He can take the dying breath of your newborn son, and weave it into a scarf to choke the life from the woman who killed him. He's an alchemist of human couture, an artist without equal or equivalent."

"Seriously?"

"Seriously. Though his wares are rarely put to good use. For this reason his business is rather shady and his prices rule out all but a handful of people."

"You're talking metaphorically, right? Either that, or this is some 'emperor's new clothes' scam I haven't heard about."

Vince put down his drink and gave Jimmy such a withering look he felt his scrotum shrivel.

"If that's what you think," said Vince. "Then our business is done. Be careful on your way out, this is a dangerous neighbourhood."

"Alright," said Jimmy. "I'm not saying that's what I think, but what you're saying is quite far out there, you have to admit."

"And yet this is the man you want to track down. Why? It's not just curiosity is it? Something violent and completely unbelievable happened to you, didn't it? I knew it the moment I saw you. That's why I let you find me. But if you're going to find the Tailor, you're going to have to start believing in him and everything he can do. You won't find him any other way."

Jimmy felt trapped by Vince's logic. It occurred to him his scepticism was a defence mechanism. The part of him that was afraid to believe, because that meant he'd have to accept everything that had happened to him.

"Okay," Jimmy said. "Tell me what I have to do."

"Meet me at 2pm tomorrow at the top of Deptford High street. Bring whatever you have for the Tailor and ten grand in cash."

"Ten Grand! I already paid you five."

"That was for your first lesson. Your second costs more"

"I don't know, ten grand's a bit steep. I can give you another five."

"You'll bring ten or I won't be there, you'll never find me again and you'll never see the Tailor. Got that?"

Jimmy's shoulders sagged and he took another sip from of Sammi to console himself. It didn't taste any better. "Yeah, I've got that," he said. "I'll see you tomorrow."

CHAPTER TWENTY-SEVEN

VINCE WAS LATE. But Jimmy expected that. He didn't know Deptford at all. It was south of the river, between Greenwich and Blackheath, the poor cousin to those well to do areas. It was supposed to be up and coming, shedding its reputation for being rough as arseholes, but Jimmy couldn't see any difference.

He felt vulnerable and out of place as he loitered at the top of the high street. The laptop, with the last surviving copy of the footage, felt unnaturally heavy in its shoulder bag. It bumped his hip as he checked his watch for the hundredth time.

Finally, Vince sauntered into view and greeted Jimmy with a simple nod. He stood at the top of the street and tilted his head at odd angles, as though he was trying to see or hear things that Jimmy couldn't.

"So, does this Tailor have a shop around here?" Jimmy asked.

Vince shook his head. "The Tailor has no fixed address. He manifests all over the city."

"So why pick a shithole like this?"

Vince gave Jimmy another withering look. "Deptford is an ancient and magical place. It calls to every visionary and mystic who lives in London."

"For real?"

"Yes, long before the Romans came and built Londinium, Deptford was here. The Knights Templar owned it for a long time. Dr John Dee, Queen Elizabeth's conjurer, visited many times with Edward Kelly. Kit Marlowe, Shakespeare's biggest rival, was sacrificed here when someone put a knife through his eye in a boarding house by the river. His bones lie in an unmarked grave, in a Templar church whose gate posts have statues of skull and crossbones. You've heard of Chaos Magick right? Born right here in Deptford, when a man named Peter J. Carroll met Ray Sherwin and founded the Illuminates of Thanateros. Many hidden paths lead here and many unseen doors might open."

"Doors to the city beneath the city?"

Vince nodded. "The most dangerous place to travel."

Vince knelt and produced a leather pouch and a strange looking rattle from his pocket. "My asson," he said holding up the rattle for Jimmy to see. The pouch contained flour, which he sprinkled on the ground, drawing an intricate pattern. Jimmy glanced around him, expecting strange looks from the passers by.

"They won't see us if we don't we look at them directly," Vince said as if he read Jimmy's mind. "No one ever notices, unless they know what they're looking for." Jimmy stopped looking about and gave Vince his full attention.

"This is a Vèvè," said Vince, pointing at the flour pattern. "To summon the Orisha Elegguá, Lord of the Crossroads, opener of doors."

"Is an Orisha like a Loa?"

"Yes, but they come from Africa, not Haiti. Elegguá manifests both as a child and an old man. You need a child's curiosity to find the city beneath the city, but you need an old man's wisdom to walk its streets."

Vince brought a dark green leaf from his pocket. It was dried and rolled into a cigar shape. He lit the leaf with a zippo. It burned rapidly, flaking to ash, giving off thick billows of smoke. Vince dropped the ash on the Vèvè and inhaled the smoke, muttering an incantation under his breath.

He grabbed the back of Jimmy's neck, and pulled his face down into the smoke. Jimmy breathed it in. It smelled resinous and tasted bitter. He wanted to retch and cough his lungs up at the same time, but he couldn't do either.

Vince let go and Jimmy reeled back. The pavement turned to rubber beneath his feet and, for a brief moment, seemed to stretch infinitely in both directions. A sudden breeze tore round the corner and hit his back, nearly knocking him off his feet. Jimmy came back to himself and the street appeared as normal once again.

The breeze became stronger and began to swirl in the space between Vince and Jimmy. It formed a tiny, freak whirlwind and lifted up the flour and ashes from the pavement, scattering them in a sudden burst that travelled ahead of them down the high street.

"What now?" said Jimmy, surprised at how strange and hollow his voice sounded.

"Now we look for an alleyway that no one can see." Vince's voice sounded deeper and even more musical, as though it was coming from some place outside of time. It felt as though Jimmy'd had this conversations hundreds of times before, but each time it had seemed completely new.

"How do we do that?"

"We've got to walk in a certain way, think in a certain way and approach it at just the right angle. We've got to let it know that we're coming and expect it to be there when we turn into it, otherwise it won't be there. And it's never in the same place, it moves around. We've got to feel it out, let it call to us, sense it come into being just as we turn. Otherwise we'll never find it."

Vince started down the street, leaning forward like a large cat on the prowl. He motioned for Jimmy to follow him. Jimmy tagged along behind, feeling a little self-conscious. Not a single person on the street noticed them, just as Vince had said.

"You must copy how I move," Vince told Jimmy, rocking back on his heels and swaying from side to side. "Do as I do and say what I say, or you'll never find the alley." Jimmy tried to copy Vince's moves, following in his wake, feeling awkward as he tried to replicate the intricate little dance steps Vince was making. The laptop bag bumped against his hip as he moved.

Vince began to chant. "Ouvrie, Ouvrie, Open for me ALL-EE-AY!"

Jimmy followed suit, joining in with the chant. "Ouvrie, Ouvrie, Open for me ALL-EE-AY!" As he danced down one side of the high street and up the other, in pursuit of Vince and in search of the Tailor, Jimmy did feel like a child playing 'follow my leader.' He hadn't lived long enough to have an old man's wisdom, he hoped he would survive the city beneath the city.

Vince tilted his head, as though he smelled something, and swung himself round on his right heel, dropping his shoulder as he did. He grabbed Jimmy's shoulder, making him turn the same way. They veered towards the space between a card shop and a halal butcher at a wild angle.

Jimmy saw the brick wall looming up in front of him. He fully expected to collide with it face first. But that never happened. One minute they were headed straight for a wall, the next they lurched into a dank little alley that wasn't there before.

The long narrow space smelled really old, not musty or rotten, just weighed down with antiquity. There was a strange flavour to the still, somnolent air, like an exotic spice that Jimmy had never tasted before.

The wall they'd thrown themselves at lay between buildings that were two stories high. The ancient brick walls of the alley stretched up on either side of them till the sky was no more than a thin grey slit above them.

"Why are the walls so high?" Jimmy said. Not the smartest question, but he was having trouble processing what just happened.

"Because of their age, this place has been here a long, long time. Cities are always built on top of older cities. The longer a place has been here, the higher the walls around it."

The ground was covered with cobble stones that stretched all the way down to a small door in the distance. It was an old wooden door that opened in two places like a stable. Hanging over the door was a large gold sign. It showed a pair of scissors with a folding rule, encircled by laurel leaves.

"What now?" said Jimmy.

"Now you go knock and we say goodbye."

"Wait, you're not coming with me?"

"You paid me to find the Tailor, that's what I've done. You didn't pay me to get involved with Mr Isimud. No amount is high enough to make me to do that."

"But I haven't got a clue what I'm doing."

"I know, and that tactic has served you pretty well so far. I have my own fate white boy and I'm no longer a part of yours."

With that Vince took a couple of steps backwards and disappeared. Jimmy had no choice but to continue down the alley to the door.

CHAPTER TWENTY-EIGHT

THE CLOSER JIMMY got to the door, the older and more marked with age it seemed. He was afraid to knock in case he put his hand through it. He reached up to the top section and rapped tentatively. Nothing happened so he knocked a little louder.

After a long pause he heard shuffling footsteps behind the door and the upper section finally opened. A short, elderly man with a long face, a little like a bloodhound's, stood behind the door.

"Can I help you?" said the man, in a gentle, almost feminine voice.

"Erm . . . Is this where the Tailor is?"

"Tailor?"

" . . . of the True Cloth."

"What does the sign say?"

"The sign? Oh you mean this?" Jimmy pointed to the large metal scissors above the door. "Well it doesn't say anything really, there are no words on it or anything."

The elderly man raised an eyebrow.

"Oh wait, it's like one of those medieval signs isn't it? Right I get you. Look, I've not really started off on the right foot here. What I really meant to say was, is the Tailor available? The Tailor of the True Cloth, because I'd really like to see him."

"I'm afraid the Tailor doesn't see anyone until the actual fitting. Have you brought the material?"

"Material? I've brought some footage, if that's what you mean." Jimmy pulled the laptop out of his bag. "It's on here. I was told to bring it to the Tailor. I'll need to show you which file it is or I could put it on a memory stick for you if you like?"

"That's quite alright, the Tailor will know exactly what is to be cut and how to stitch it."

"Well I don't want him to cut it, unless he's like an editor or something, it's just that I was told . . . I mean asked to . . . actually I'm not certain what I want him to do with it."

"That's quite alright, everything will be undertaken just as it should be," said the man taking the laptop from Jimmy. "Now if you'd be good enough to turn around slowly for me I'll take your measurements."

"Don't you need a measuring tape or something?" said Jimmy, executing a slow twirl for the man.

"No, my eyes are more accurate than any ruler, and you dress to the left I see. Now, if you'll be good enough to wait here a moment I'll take the material to the Tailor and come back with a fee."

Jimmy waited in the alley outside the door for ten minutes until the man returned with a six figure fee that was almost the exact asking price of Sam's apartment.

"That's a lot of money," Jimmy said. "Just what is he going to do with the footage?"

"As I said everything will be explained to you in good time. Simply return here in ten days' time with the fee."

"It's probably going to take me that long to raise it."

"That is most serendipitous then. I believe you can find your own way out."

"Wait, how will I find you again."

"Just come to the same part of town, we'll be here."

"But what if I can't . . . y'know, locate the alley or something?"

"Then you won't be able to collect your wares. The Tailor, on the other hand will still expect his fee, and will most certainly find a way to collect it. Good day."

With that the elderly man shut the upper section of the door and Jimmy heard his shuffling footsteps disappear into whatever lay beyond it.

Jimmy turned from the door and within five steps was at the mouth of the alley. This left him very disoriented. He was sure the walk down the alley had been much longer. He looked back over his shoulder to check the distance but saw only the brick wall between the card shop and the butchers. All trace of the alley had gone.

In a brief moment of panic, Jimmy wondered if Vince had drugged him? Was the smoke he'd made Jimmy inhale some sort of hallucinogen? Had he imagined the whole encounter? Was it all an elaborate con to steal his laptop?

No, that was crazy, Vince had just gotten fifteen grand out of Jimmy. Why would he want to steal his laptop? Unless Vince was the one who killed Ashkan and his men and he needed to retrieve the laptop. That didn't make any sense though. Vince could have just killed him and taken the laptop. Why set up such an elaborate prank?

Jimmy was just getting paranoid, and who could blame him after everything he'd been through. Even still he couldn't afford to lose it, not when he was so close. He'd found the Tailor and given him the footage, just as Melissa had instructed. He wasn't going to fuck up this time. He really was coming back for her, just as he promised.

CHAPTER TWENTY-NINE

TEN DAYS LATER, Jimmy felt just as awkward on the streets of Deptford. It wasn't that he still thought the place a dump, with its cheesy discount stores and its raucous collection of winos. It was more that he was carrying a briefcase containing hundreds of thousands of pounds, from the sale of Sam's apartment. The estate agent had advised him to hold out for a higher price, but Jimmy had needed a quick sale, so he'd settled.

Without Vince, Jimmy wasn't sure he could find the alley again. He couldn't do any of that voodoo stuff that Vince had done, drawing on the ground in flour and ash. He didn't have any of that weird leaf smoke to inhale either. He was just going to have to wing it and hope he could remember enough to get back to the Tailor.

Jimmy moved up the high street to the spot where he last found the alley, doing his best to replicate what Vince had done, dancing in a half-hearted manner. He chanted:

"Ouvrie, Ouvrie, Open for me ALL-EE-AY!" under his breath.

The closer he got to the spot, the more self-conscious Jimmy became. He didn't want to draw attention to himself. He knew he looked ridiculous skipping down the street trying to remember all the moves Vince had thrown. He felt like an embarrassing uncle getting up to dance at a teenage party.

Finally Jimmy reached the spot between the card shop and the Halal Butcher. He swung round on his heel, with his right shoulder down, and very nearly knocked his teeth out on the brick wall. It was only because he panicked and put his hand up at the last minute, that he didn't do himself a real injury.

Jimmy stepped back from the wall, danced up the street, turned round and headed back to the spot. The second time he lunged at it he smacked his shoulder into the wall, sending a jarring pain down his arm and along the top of his back.

The third time he tried, he lost his balance and ended up on all fours with his face pressed against the brick wall, in the same spot where a dog had relieved itself. Jimmy stood and used a tissue to wipe his cheek.

Three guys came out of the Halal Butchers to see what Jimmy was playing at. They stood by the door with their arms crossed and their feet apart, weighing Jimmy up with guarded but hostile expressions. Jimmy grabbed his briefcase and started walking down the street towards the station.

He obviously wasn't going to find the entrance to the alley in that spot again. Hopefully it would appear to him somewhere else on the High Street, or he'd have to start looking further abroad.

Jimmy's cheeks were burning with shame. He felt exposed; not only by his strange behaviour, but also by the huge amount of money he was carrying. He thought every eye would be on him for his ridiculous display, but the reverse was the case. People were making a studied effort to ignore him. It struck Jimmy that this might be the answer.

Someone who's getting noticed too much is never going to slip quietly into an alley few people know exists. The alley, or its inhabitants, take great care to avoid attention. To slip into the alley Jimmy would have to make himself equally invisible and unnoticed. This must have been what Vince meant when he said you had to approach it in the right way.

The way people avoided his eye made Jimmy realise Vince's chants and movements were a way of diverting other people's attention, as much as willing the alley into being. In a city like London, especially in an area like Deptford, people went out of their way not to notice other people, especially if they were acting in a strange or embarrassing way.

Jimmy started to rock back and forth on his heels as he walked, just as Vince had shown him, stopping every now and then to alter his direction or take a few steps backwards for no apparent reason. He pictured the cobbled stones of the alley and started to walk as though they were underfoot. He pictured the alley and listed every detail he could recall under his breath, remembering the rhythms Vince had used when he chanted.

Jimmy spotted a small Chinese supermarket up ahead, right next to a charity shop and he knew that, if he played things right, he would find the alley there. It was an intuitive, almost physical knowledge that was also a warning. If he played things wrong, he would never find the alley again and all his efforts would be in vain.

As Jimmy passed the Chinese supermarket his eyes kept darting left, hoping to see the alley, but there was no sign of it. He knew he would have to make a leap of faith and just walk right into it, but in the right way and at the right angle.

As he passed the mini supermarket Jimmy swivelled round on his left heel and dived at the wall between the two shops. To his alarm, he realised his right shoulder was too high and too far forwards and he may not have time to fix it. He dropped the shoulder and lunged at the painted bricks between the two shops.

To his delight Jimmy found himself standing on the cobbled stones of the alley.

CHAPTER THIRTY

THE ANCIENT WALLS sloped upwards on either side of Jimmy. Ahead lay the wooden door and the metal sign. The air tasted more exotic than he remembered, but it didn't smell as old. Jimmy had the sense of having crossed a threshold. He'd entered the city beneath the city of his own volition. There was no going back. He'd committed himself to a course of action and had to accept whatever came after this.

The sound of his feet on the cobblestones sounded muted the closer he got to the door, as though coming from a long way away. He lifted his hand to knock but the top section was opened before he could.

The short elderly man peered out at him. "We've been expecting you for a while now," he said.

"Yeah, I err, had a bit of trouble finding the place again."

"We'd almost given up on seeing you."

"You're not the easiest place to find."

"There are many good reasons for that."

The elderly man opened the rest of the door and motioned, with a gracious bow, for Jimmy to come in. Jimmy stepped into a small antechamber with no windows, lit by a single gas lamp on a wooden countertop. Lengths of cloth and baskets of wool sat against the opposite wall. Several of the baskets were moving. Maybe there were mice or rats in them, or something Jimmy didn't want to know about.

"If you'd be good enough to wait here," said the elderly man, "I'll tell the Tailor you've arrived."

He went through a door at the far side of the antechamber and closed it behind him. Jimmy heard muffled voices, and then the elderly man's shuffling footsteps.

"Please come inside," said the elderly man, popping his head around the door. "The Tailor will see you now."

The room beyond could not have been more of a contrast. It was expansive and filled with light from a large window that took up most of the ceiling. There was a huge wooden bench in the centre of the room made from delicately carved mahogany.

Half of the bench top was covered with crushed red velvet. Laid out on the velvet were more blades and cutting implements than Jimmy knew existed, neatly displayed in elaborate leather belts. Their designs were so strange he could only guess at what half of them did.

Against the long wall opposite, was a row of tailor's dummies. Each one a different size, resembling every human body imaginable. Several resembled no human body Jimmy could imagine.

As interesting as the setting was, the room was dominated by a tall, thin man with a long, angular face that reminded Jimmy of a crescent moon. His thick moustache and pointy goatee only added to this impression. He had blazing brown eyes that made Jimmy hesitant to meet his gaze. His charcoal suit was of such a faultless cut, it seemed to tailor the very light that fell on it, so as to appear more perfect. The effect was mesmerising.

Next to the Tailor was one of his dummies. This one was covered with a cloth. Jimmy's heart began to beat faster the minute he spotted it. He couldn't believe the anticipation he felt.

"Are you the err, the Tailor of the True Cloth?" Jimmy said.

The Tailor gave a short, formal nod.

"I'm Ji . . . "

The Tailor held up his hand to silence Jimmy. "No names please, it makes our business so much easier."

"Do you really have the kind of mad skills they say you have?"

The Tailor's brow furrowed with slight irritation. "Why on earth would you go to such lengths to find me, and pay so much for my services if you thought I didn't?"

"Right, no, sorry, I wasn't trying to be rude. It's just all a bit much to take in, you know?"

Jimmy pointed to the covered dummy. "Is that . . . my God, did you really . . . have you made a suit out of the footage I brought you? For real?"

"No, I haven't made a suit, I've made a robe. The garment must suit the material from which it's fashioned. A robe is more fitting to its ancient origins."

"Ancient origins? It's a snuff movie, it can't be more than two years old."

The Tailor raised an eyebrow in disbelief. "A snuff movie? You think that's what you brought me?"

"Well yeah, isn't it?"

The Tailor let out a short sigh and put his hand to his forehead. He closed his eyes for a moment as though he was marshalling the patience to deal with Jimmy's ignorance. Jimmy did not know how to respond.

"It is most certainly not a snuff movie. It's something far more deadly than you obviously realise. I see now it was a mistake to have made this for you and for that reason I cannot allow you to take it."

"What?! Now wait a minute, you have no idea what I've been through to get this to you."

"I can guess."

Jimmy held up the briefcase. "I brought a small fortune. Do you know how difficult it was to get the bank to hand this over in cash?"

"It's never easy to get a bank to hand anything over. It's why I seldom deal with them."

"Please, you can't do this. Not when I'm so close. It's not for me, there's this woman you see . . . "

"There often is."

"No, it's not like that. She's trapped in the film, in the footage or whatever you think it is, or at least her spirit is, and she needs to me to help . . . to come back for her."

"Come back for her?"

"It's complicated, but she needs me. I have to help her, you don't understand . . . "

"No, it's you who doesn't understand and that's why I cannot give you the garment."

"Then make me understand, please," Jimmy could not believe the desperation in his voice. "You have to help me. I'm all she's got."

The Tailor said nothing. He stood and scrutinised Jimmy for what felt like ages, making him feel like a badly turned hem in need of re-stitching.

"Very well," he said, after the longest pause. "But I will have to open your eyes to many things, and the world will never seem the same once I have. Are you prepared for that?"

"My world hasn't been the same since I came into contact with that footage, or whatever it is. How much worse could it get?"

"Let us see," said the Tailor.

CHAPTER THIRTY-ONE

THE TAILOR LIFTED the cover on the dummy and reached underneath. Jimmy couldn't see exactly what he was doing, but his quick, dextrous fingers seemed to be unpicking something.

"The robe is unfinished in one area, as befits the material I was working with," said the Tailor. "I can only apologise about that, but I'm afraid it couldn't be avoided. I'll explain why in good time."

The Tailor produced a long thin thread from under the cover. It was multi-coloured and appeared to be glowing, or perhaps shining would be a more appropriate term. The pattern on the slender thread seemed to be moving and constantly changing, almost as if it were alive.

"Just as the entire history of the universe can be learned from a single molecule, if you know how to read it. So the history of a whole garment can be found in a single thread. Now, in order to open your eyes, I'm going to have to ask you to close them."

Jimmy shut his eyes as the Tailor moved behind him. He felt the Tailor reach around and place the thread over his eyelids. Then he pulled it taut and tied it behind Jimmy's head.

"Ow, that's actually a bit tight," said Jimmy.

"It's supposed to be."

Jimmy felt the pressure of the thread on his eyeballs. But more than that, the glowing, multiple colours of the thread's pattern shone through his eyelids and hit the back of his retina. This created huge explosions of colour behind his closed eyes. The colours were amorphous to begin with, but soon formed intricate, ever shifting patterns, like a kaleidoscope.

The sensation reminded Jimmy of car rides with his parents when he was a child on holiday. The road to the cottage by the sea they always rented, wound beneath a canopy of branches. On sunny days, with the top of the car down, Jimmy would lie back with his eyes closed and let the sunlight play on his face as it broke through the branches.

The patterns he saw then, were similar to the patterns he saw now. This was more intense though, like rubbing your eyes while peaking on acid. The patterns he saw became more complex and started to form images. Fleeting at first and not very clear, the images became clearer and more frequent. He saw a sacrificial blade with a jewel encrusted hilt, an engraved silver chalice and a wall frieze with cuneiform and Mesopotamian deities like the ones he'd read about.

Eventually the images merged into one great vista. As if from a great height, Jimmy saw a fertile plane bordered on both sides by mighty rivers.

As the vision came into view it became clearer and clearer. Jimmy was seeing with a sharpness and precision his eyes could never normally muster. He could look for miles with pin point accuracy, picking out the tiniest blade of grass, like a bird of prey.

THE FINAL CUT

A small, ancient settlement came into view on the lower banks of the left hand river. Jimmy began to approach the settlement at a rapid pace. On the very outskirts of the settlement were simple makeshift structures, they soon gave way to crude stone and clay buildings. These buildings were thrown up around large city walls that covered a great distance.

The intricate stone walls were high and had many gates, most of them surrounded by ornate stone carvings. Beyond the gates were paved streets and multi storey municipal buildings. Statues of mythical creatures, half man and half bull, half woman and half bird, dotted the many plazas.

"Tell me what you see," said the Tailor, whispering in Jimmy's ear.

"I'm in a city I think, it's not one I recognise, it's very old. I'm guessing it's somewhere in the Middle East."

"It's the ancient city of Uruk. It was built nearly four thousand years before the birth of Christ."

"Right in the centre of the city is what looks like a pyramid with the top half cut off. It's terraced and there are steps running up each side which lead to the top terrace, where there's a huge temple. It's blinding white and incredibly high."

"What you're seeing is a ziggurat, one of the first ever built."

Jimmy moved towards the ziggurat at a high speed, swooping down to the temple. He flinched as it hurtled up towards him but he passed though the walls as if they weren't there. Inside the temple, the sun streamed through the wooden lattices that filled the high windows. The gloom that filled the ground level was lifted by flaming bowls of oil on high metal stands.

In the centre of the temple, on a set of stone steps that led to an altar, was a small crowd of people.

"Tell me who you see."

"Erm, there's a short guy with thinning black hair and a long plaited beard, right at the bottom of some steps. He's talking and waving his arms around as though he's acting something out."

"That is Mr Isimud, or simply Isimud as he was known then, named for the two faced messenger of the god Enki. Mere moments before he becomes immortal."

"At the top of the steps there's a tall woman in a long white robe with an ornate head dress, it looks like it's made out of pure gold, it's so delicate."

"That's a High Priestess of the temple. An exalted position that gave her more power than any woman has ever wielded since."

"Seriously, you're telling me she had more power than women do today?"

"Infinitely more. When you've lived as long as I have, you learn there are vast chunks of the past that humans purposefully forget or ignore. The Priestess is not a woman you'd want to upset, and she's sentenced Isimud to death for Heresy."

"Would that be the . . . err, Qu'rm Saddic Heresy? Is it really that old?"

"Older than man if its adherents are to be believed, and hated by every religion throughout history. The ancients feared that, if left unchecked, it would alter the consciousness of everyone alive. Isimud was proven a believer and that meant certain death."

"So what is he doing if she's sentenced him to death?"

"He's telling her, and everyone assembled a story, in return for a pardon. The Priestess is known for being wise, and sometimes lenient, so she's granted his audacious request. If the story pleases everyone, he may be set free, or at least escape death."

But the story wasn't pleasing everyone. In fact it didn't seem to be pleasing anyone. Many people were gathered on the steps. Towards the bottom were soldiers, in loincloths with spears and plaited beards. They were all simmering with barely concealed rage. Above them were bald, clean-shaven priests, more priestesses and other temple dignitaries, all in robes and headdresses—none so ornate and startling as those of the High Priestess though. Each of them looked appalled by what Isimud was saying. Only the High Priestess remained impassive and unmoved.

"What story is he telling them?"

"It's a version of Inanna's journey to the underworld, but a much older version than anyone in Uruk had ever heard. Isimud's version was more ferocious, more violent and more steeped in blood than any that has been told since. This, like every truth in Isimud's heresy, made it incredibly dangerous."

"I don't think he's going to get his pardon."

"He won't need it."

Isimud seemed to have reached a high point of his tale. He became more animated and his expression turned ferocious. The soldiers levelled their spears ready to impale him. The priests threw up their arms in outrage. The priestesses turned away in disgust. Even the High Priestess was perturbed. She lowered her eyelids, until her eyes were glowering slits, and she set her jaw.

Isimud continued unabashed. Several of the priestesses ran crying from the steps and at least half the priests followed them. The soldiers began to advance on Isimud, ready to run him through right there.

The air above Isimud's head began to thicken and roil, as though it had taken on a substance all of its own, like lowering bodiless clouds. The arms and heads of strange creatures began to appear in the air.

"Something's trying to break through into the temple. Blurred figures, I've seen them before. They were in the footage."

"They're Anunnaki."

"What?"

"Anunnaki, Sumerian sky deities, servants of the sky god An. They're similar to what people today call angels, only Anunnaki are far more deadly. Like the angels, many of the Anunnaki fell from grace. Some left the sky to dwell on Earth and others the underworld. Some became judges, such as the Anunnaki who kept Inanna in Hell."

"What are they doing in the temple?"

"The story attracted their attention. Isimud wasn't telling the story to please the High Priestess. He was telling it to summon the Anunnaki. They were so entranced by his telling, they decided to make his story their home and inhabit it."

Isimud kept talking, his gesticulations becoming wilder. The Anunnaki swirled around in the thick air overhead and then darted after the priests and priestesses who were fleeing the steps. More appeared, conjured by Isimud's tale, and seized the advancing soldiers. The priests who remained on the steps fell to their knees and tried to cover their ears. This didn't save them.

The Anunnaki fell on every member of the retinue. The soldiers fought them, so did some of the priests and priestesses, others just begged and pleaded for their lives. None of their efforts came to anything. The Anunnaki were implacably lethal.

The blurred figures didn't just flay the skin off the entire retinue. Nor did they stop at tearing out their innards and pounding them into liquid. They didn't rest until they'd eviscerated every ounce of flesh on the victim's bodies and then ground their skeletal frames into brittle, white bone dust.

There was no anger, nor even malice, in the the Anunnaki's ferocious attack. It was as if they were solemnly enacting a sacred duty.

"They're slaughtering everyone," said Jimmy, jerking his head around, unable to look away, or even close his eyes to the vision that was unfolding in front of him. "What are they doing that for?"

"They're acting out of kindness. It's an act of devotion, to the divinity within all humans, to scourge the flesh they hate so much, rending it, tearing it and destroying it utterly."

"But why?"

"Because human flesh is the cruellest part of the prison we call the material world. The Anunnaki are also devotees of the 'faith that came before man,' that's why Isimud's tale attracted them. They loathe the material world and see it as a trap for the souls of humanity. They believe the souls of every living creature are a part of the one true God who created the whole universe but became enslaved by it. Like a beam of light shining through a prism, the world of matter refracted God when He entered it, and held Him powerless within all the living things He produced. As a consequence, all life is suffering, because living distracts each of us from our true divinity and the fact that we are all part of one God who is imprisoned by His own creation, cut off from His greater self and experiencing Himself individually."

The High Priestess, who'd remained untouched until now, finally broke. She screwed her fingers into her ears and turned to flee from the head of the steps to a small chamber behind. She never made it. What the Anunnaki did to her was worse than anything they'd done to her retinue. They seemed all the more sorrowful because of this.

"Oh my God, what they're doing to her."

"Is out of love, for her true divinity."

"They're doing all this because of the story Isimud's telling?"

"They have come to inhabit it, to make it their home."

"But why would they want to inhabit his tale?"

"It's where all deities go eventually. When their temples have fallen to ruin, and all their worshipers have died, all that remains are the stories once told of them. This story allowed the Anunnaki to walk among the living while it was still told."

Isimud dropped to his knees, sweat dripped from his forehead and his chest. He rubbed his throat as if it hurt but he kept on talking.

"Isimud looks almost done."

"He's afraid that once he ends his story the Anunnaki will have nothing to hold them and they'll turn on him."

Time sped up and Jimmy watched Isimud slowly weaken. His throat getting rawer, his voice cracking, becoming a croaked whisper. His body slumping into an exhausted heap on the temple floor as the Anunnaki lurked overhead.

Finally Isimud rolled over onto his back, his voice just about to give out, his face resigned to his fate. Then as his voice trailed away to nothing, a dim thought could be seen shining within his dull eyes, bringing back a spark of hope on the cusp of death.

Isimud seemed to get a tiny lease of life and a sly expression stole across his face. He found a new twist to the tale that resuscitated him. The Anunnaki stopped churning the air above him and became still, disappearing calmly into the faint echo of Isimud's last words.

"The Anunnaki have gone . . . how? How did he do that?"

"He found a way to finish the story without ending it."

"What do you mean?"

"He concocted a way to avoid ending the story, even though he stopped telling it. The story was meant to stay his execution, but by refusing it an ending he's held off his death ever since."

Isimud got up from the floor and left the temple by a back entrance. The blood of the High Priestess and her slaughtered retinue had almost faded to nothing. Time raced forward and Jimmy was lifted up and out of the temple. He looked down at the plain from on high once again. He watched as other cities flourished along the banks of the two rivers and also further inland.

Uruk's power and influence was eclipsed by younger cities like Nippur, Nineveh and eventually Babylon. Their armies grew larger, their riches greater and their territories spread over the millennia. Isimud remained alive the whole time.

"I don't understand. Why doesn't Isimud die?"

"Why don't the names of story tellers like Homer, Shakespeare or Dickens ever die? Because their stories keep them alive. A story inhabited by immortal beings will keep the story teller alive indefinitely."

The vision changed, it moved to the back room of a tavern in Babylon. The tavern was owned by Isimud, no one but him knew of the backroom. He was showing four jaded aristocrats into it, they acted with patronising disdain, but they were expectant, as if some particular entertainment had been promised.

Isimud opened a large silver chest and took out some oversized clay tablets with cuneiform writing and grotesque images. The aristocrats crowed round the tablets, their gleeful expressions soon turned to frowns of disgust and they began to cry out in outrage.

The shadowy, blurred figures of the Anunnaki were released from the tablets and the aristocrats were released from the prison of their flesh. The vision moved closer to the tablets until they filled Jimmy's sight. The hardened clay became soft and insubstantial, changing shape and reforming itself into a papyrus scroll filled with hieroglyphics.

Isimud was showing the scroll to a band of travelling merchants who smiled avariciously and rubbed their hands together. They were not smiling by the time the Anunnaki appeared. Jimmy's sight was filled with the scroll when they were done and he saw it change shape once again into a single edition book that looked like it had come fresh off a Gutenberg press. This one was being placed into the eager hands of some Bavarian fur trappers, who did not manage to keep their own skins after they read it.

The book went through many different editions, changing paper, binding and language until it changed shape altogether and became a single reel of super 8 film, viewed in many smoke filled backrooms, by men with rolled shirt sleeves and seamy foreheads. In time the film became a VHS cassette and then . . .

CHAPTER THIRTY-TWO

JIMMY TOOK HOLD of the thread and pulled it off his eyelids.

"The footage . . . it's the story. It's thousands of years old."

"Yes it is. Like all good fiction it has changed and adapted itself to the latest medium. The story has slowly evolved so it can most effectively prey on the select few who encounter it. The type of twisted individuals who seek out such material."

"You haven't explained about the ending though. Why would the story keep going just because it was open ended? I like open endings."

"That might be your biggest problem as a film maker. A story without an ending lacks the proper shape or form, it insults its audience and plagues their mind because it lacks resolution."

"Real life doesn't have any resolution or neat endings."

"Fiction isn't real life," said the Tailor, as though he were explaining something to a child. "When you tell a story you are setting a contract with your audience. You don't say to them 'Let me tell you something that happened in real life,' you say, 'Let me tell you a story.' People look to stories to give them the things that real life doesn't."

"Such as?"

"In real life your problems are rarely resolved, you don't get closure on the situations or relationships that have most impact on your life. Your father never explains why he didn't say how proud you made him. Your ex-wife never apologies for cheating on you repeatedly. Bad people aren't punished for their crimes and good people go unrewarded for their virtue. We look to stories to give us the closure and the resolution we so desperately crave, so we can deal with our problems and move on in a way that real life doesn't allow."

"But it's the lack of an ending that kept this story alive, you just said so."

"But not in a healthy way, not because it's told and retold. This story exists as an abomination of a story's natural life. It is an undead tale that has to feed off the blood of its listeners to continue to exist and in doing so it grants its teller an obtuse immortality."

"It didn't take me or Sam when we watched it, why is that?"

"Maybe it had other plans for you. Did you watch the footage to the very end?"

"No, I had my eyes closed."

"That might have saved your life. The story tests you, pushes you beyond the limits of your endurance. It's waiting for you to weaken, to reach the point you're no longer insensitive to its atrocities. That's when you can't help but identify with the victims and you join them. It takes you as soon as you can't bear to watch to the bitter end."

"Because there is no end."

"Exactly, and there is no end to the victim's suffering."

"Why, what happens to them?"

"They become part of the story, they feed it, living through their murder and torture over and over again."

"Is that what's happened to Melissa?"

"Melissa?"

"The girl I'm trying to help."

"I don't know, there is someone in the story who's not like the other victims. Tell me, have you seen her outside of the story?"

"Yes, yes I have. I actually cast her in a movie I was making."

"So she's manifesting, I thought as much. That would make her a character, not a victim."

"What's the difference?"

"She's more active and important to the course of the story."

"But how was I able to see her, and touch her?"

"Many people interact with their favourite characters. A child visiting Santa at the mall, for instance, or a fan meeting an actor, or a cosplayer in character. Some characters get a hold on our imaginations and cross over from fiction into the real world."

"So Melissa got a hold on our imaginations and crossed over into our world, but how? By taking over someone else's body and making them look like her?"

"There are some mysteries it's best not to dwell on."

Jimmy thought about the confused girl he'd seen outside the studio when he'd pursued Melissa. Then he thought about some of the things Melissa might have done, and what could have happened to Sam, and he didn't want to think about it anymore. The Tailor was probably right.

"How did she get to be a character though?" said Jimmy. "I mean she's a real person, or she was."

"All characters are partly based on real people. Authors put real people into their stories all the time."

"So you think that's what Isimud did to her?"

The Tailor nodded.

"Vince says Isimud knows I'm looking for him."

"I don't much care for Vince, but he's seldom wrong."

"How can I get her out of the footage, how can I rescue her?"

"The first thing you need to do is locate Mr Isimud."

"That's why I came to you. Do you know where I can find him?"

"Not all things are known to me, but I do have something that will lead you to him."

The Tailor indicated the covered dummy.

"Can I see it?" said Jimmy. "The robe you made, from the footage."

The Tailor smiled, pleased with the anticipation he saw on Jimmy's face. He took hold of the covering with a flourish, then paused. It was a moment of high drama, akin to unveiling a major work of art. Jimmy leaned forward and the Tailor finally revealed his handiwork.

It was impossible to look directly at the robe, because it was hard for the brain to understand what it was seeing. It was an object that had no place in the limited dimensions of Jimmy's experience.

It was easier to take the robe in by not looking

directly at it, or by focusing on a single detail, such as a shot from the footage that played about the hem. The Tailor hadn't just woven a bunch of shots together and made a static garment, nor did the footage play out over the surface of the robe, like a screen. It seemed that the Tailor had taken the whole experience of watching the footage and made it into a single item of clothing. Everything you saw or felt while viewing the footage was all there simultaneously, in a synaesthetic totality, woven into every strand of the cloth.

"As I said before, this is a purposefully unfinished work," said the Tailor. "I was not able to finish the cut. I regret this, and apologise, but I am bound by the integrity of the material I work with, and it would not have been possible to create the garment if I had finished it."

The Tailor indicated a small section at the back where the robe wasn't hemmed but seemed to trail off, almost into another dimension of space.

"How will this lead me to Mr Isimud?"

"First you put it on, then you go wherever it takes you. It will know exactly how to find him. It is part of his story, so it will always return to him."

"Part of his story? I thought the footage was the story."

"This is only the latest incarnation, the visible part of the story if you will, like the tip of an iceberg showing above the water. The rest of the story resides with its teller and the footage will want to join it, so it will take you there."

"But what happens when I get there? What's this Mr Isimud going to do? I mean if he trapped Melissa in his story and made her a character, he's not just going to hand her over is he?"

"Have you ever read a story where that happens?"

"No, but this isn't a story, it's actually happening."

"Are you entirely sure of that?"

"Are you saying I'm hallucinating all of this?"

"No that's not what I'm saying at all, I'm asking what you know about fiction?"

"You mean if I want to free a character from a story, I have to follow the rules of fiction."

"And what rules usually apply to fictional rescues from Hell?"

"Wait, you said she was trapped in a story, not Hell."

"Both Heaven and Hell are stories that we tell ourselves. They're ways of coping with our mortality and what comes after."

"I suppose you're right, that's why we tell tales about descents into the underworld isn't it?"

"Yes it is."

"So if I'm going into the underworld to rescue someone, the rules are that I need to accomplish a task or face an ordeal. Like Eurydice, she was being guarded by the monster Cerberus, Orpheus put it to sleep with his lyre, so she could escape."

"And what monster is guarding Melissa?

"There isn't one."

"Are you sure?"

"Unless you count the story itself. Vince called it a monster. I mean you said it was killing people because it didn't have an ending and it's gone and trapped Melissa, but how do you slay a story?"

"How do you slay anything? You give it an ending of course. A fit and proper ending, one that ties up every loose end."

"That's easier said than done."

"Yes it is. There are many ways to finish a story, but only one true way to end it. Every other attempt at finishing is a misstep, a distraction and will not lead to the tale's proper ending. You must find the one true way to end it and administer the final cut."

"I've never been good with endings though, that's why I avoid conclusive ones."

"You need to find whatever it is that stops you from ending things then."

"And if I do?"

"You'll succeed in your quest, your lady will get what she wants."

"And me?"

"You will also be saved. But be warned, the best stories never follow the rules quite how you'd expect."

CHAPTER THIRTY-THREE

CAN I PUT it on now? Jimmy said. The Tailor nodded. Jimmy removed his clothes and the Tailor placed the robe around his shoulders.

It didn't feel like anything he'd ever worn before. The robe wasn't heavy as such, it just had the grave weight of a terrible tale about tragic events. It didn't feel like fabric against his skin, it had the substance of stories, as though there was now a barrier of fiction standing between him and the world and Jimmy could rewrite himself endlessly, changing the way he was perceived and how he interacted with everything around him.

The elderly man wheeled out a full length mirror and placed it in front of Jimmy. The robe in the reflection was even more difficult to look at and even busier to the eye.

"Does it really look like that on me?" said Jimmy. "It seems larger and formless, like it's growing all the time."

"That's because stories are only mirrored by other stories," said the Tailor. "What you're seeing is every other story in which this story is reflected, including, I might add, your own."

There seemed to be tiny, shimmering lines

radiating from the robe, covering his face, hands and legs, like a heat haze. As each line passed over his face, it was transformed, showing the image of another character who might have his role in the story. This made his face look like a constantly changing, composite picture of characters from throughout history.

"I take it you're satisfied with your purchase?" said the Tailor.

"Yes," said Jimmy. "Yes, I think this will do nicely."

The Tailor nodded to the elderly man who stepped away from the mirror and picked up the briefcase.

Jimmy felt the robe take hold of his imagination and start to bend his thoughts. It was similar to the feeling he got when a script idea grabbed him and he was powerless to do anything but sit down and write, giving himself over to the idea until he had the whole story down. Only this feeling was a hundred times stronger, and a hundred times more obsessive.

The robe had gripped Jimmy, like a story he couldn't put down, and he let himself be carried along with it. He left the Tailor and the elderly man without a second glance. He was like a writer in thrall to his work, he was going to let the tale take him wherever it wanted to go.

Jimmy sensed something more of the robe though. It was demanding that he choose a role. He was wearing make believe as his mantle, and he had to become a character to do so, to pick out a mask to present to the world. He didn't need to deliberate over this. He was Dumuzi, in search of his Inanna.

CHAPTER THIRTY-FOUR

JIMMY MARCHED OUT of the shop, up the cobbled alley and out onto the high street. He came to a mini cab office, pushed open the glass door and walked into the waiting room. There was cracked linoleum on the floor and faded blue paint on the walls, the skirting board was scuffed. The whole place seemed dirty, run down and neglected. A bored black guy with a big afro sat behind a grimy window that opened onto the despatch office.

"Help you?" the guy said without looking up.

"I'd like a cab please," said Jimmy. His voice sounded odd to him, as though it were a chorus of voices all speaking in unison. He was many characters speaking at once.

It occurred to Jimmy that he was connecting with the world around him through a filter of myth. People talk about getting immersed in a story, but they have no idea what that really means. Jimmy knew what it meant; he was clothed in a story. Everything he said, and everything he touched turned to fiction.

"Where you going?" said the guy.

"Through the seven gates and into the Underworld."

"Seven Sisters, that's in Haringey innit? On the Victoria line."

"I don't want the underground, I want the Underworld."

For the first time the guy looked up and saw Jimmy. He blinked, did a double take, and then his eyes glazed over as though he were falling under the spell of the story in which Jimmy was dressed.

"The Underworld, sorry mate, must've misheard you innit. I'll get someone on it straight away. What's the name?"

"Dumuzi."

"Dumb Uzi, is that like a street tag or something?"

"No, I'm a shepherd who married a goddess and became the king of Uruk."

The guy's mouth fell open and he got to his feet out of respect. "Well hell, why didn't you say? We've never had royalty in here before."

The guy picked up his radio receiver. "Dennis, yeah bruv, got one for ya. And get this, he's a king . . . no a real life king . . . I don't know somewhere foreign. He wants to go to the Underworld innit . . . nah, mate, I said Underworld . . . yeah Underworld, seriously . . . okay, I'll send him right out."

The guy left the office and came into the waiting area. "Here, let me get that door for you." He pointed to a car across the road. "That silver Toyota right outside, your majesty. Dennis the driver will take care of you."

Jimmy left the office and saw a short fat guy, in a brown shirt and blue pants, leaning against a silver Toyota. "Dennis?" he said.

"Yeah, so you're a king right?"

"Yes, of the city of Uruk."

"That somewhere abroad?"

"It's in the land of Sumer."

"Thought so, please have a seat, your highness."

Dennis held open the passenger door. Jimmy climbed into the front seat while Dennis squeezed himself behind the wheel. He smelled as though he hadn't had a bath in weeks. "Where to, your highness?" said Dennis.

"Just start driving," said Jimmy. "I'll tell you where to go." Jimmy didn't actually know where they were going. He was relying on the robe to guide him. It was like an intuition you don't know you have, until it suddenly kicks in. Jimmy would feel a mental tug in a certain direction and he'd tell Dennis to turn down a street, almost at random, with no pattern he or Dennis could guess at. He was navigating the city beneath the city and there were no maps for that.

Finally they came out of the Blackwall tunnel.

"So," said Dennis. "This Underworld, it's a club, yeah?"

"It's the domain of Erishkigal, Queen of the Underworld."

"Queen of the Underworld, so it's a gay club then?"

"She was married to Gugalanna, but he's dead now."

"Right, that's a pity."

"She eats clay, drinks water, and her sexual appetite is insatiable. When the death god Nergal visited her they copulated for six whole days and when he left, on the seventh, she was still not satisfied."

"So she likes to party, sounds like my kinda woman."

They headed up Commercial Street and turned left onto City Road. The route was just beginning to make sense to Jimmy when they took off down a few side streets and came out in a mews just around the back of the Angel.

"Pull up here," said Jimmy as they approached an underground car park.

Dennis stopped the car. "That'll be twenty seven pounds thirty five, your highness."

Jimmy picked a ball point pen off the floor of the cab. "This is my golden sceptre of office," he said, and as he spoke the shimmering lines that his robe gave off flowed over the pen, changing it into a carved golden rod. "It will cause your crops to flourish, your cattle to multiply and your seed to be ever fruitful in the belly of your woman."

Dennis's eyes bugged out of his head. "Can I sell it on eBay?"

"With this sceptre, you can rule eBay."

"Shit!"

Jimmy opened the door of the car and started to climb out. Dennis was still staring at the sceptre with awe when his radio crackled into life. "Hey Dennis, when you're finished with that king I got another ride for you."

"You can stick that right up your arse."

"Come again?"

"You heard me, stick it up your arse. I rule eBay now. I'm gonna be fucking rich."

Jimmy shut the door and headed towards the car park. He'd begun to learn what most politicians, media tycoons and business leaders already knew. People will believe, or do, anything you want them to, so long as you tell them a powerful enough story. Jimmy was wearing that story.

The robe pulled Jimmy towards the staircase in the far corner of the car park. He went down seven flights of dank concrete steps that smelled of urine.

At the bottom of the seventh flight was a steel door with a covered window set into it. Jimmy banged on the door. The window cover slid back and a shaven-headed man looked out at him.

"What?" he said.

"I'm here to see Mr Isimud," Jimmy said.

"Fuck off, he ain't seeing no-one."

The window began to slide shut. Jimmy reached over and stopped it with his hand. "Tell him I have ascended from my throne dressed in my shining 'me-garments.'"

The eyes of the man behind the window glazed over as the story got to work on him. "Why didn't you say, mate. Hold up a minute."

Jimmy heard the sound of bolts being pulled back and the door creaked open. The guy, who was wearing a grey tracksuit and white trainers, motioned for him to come inside. There was a dark corridor beyond the door that ended in a small vestibule.

Inside the vestibule, a bald bloke with a thick moustache sat behind a desk lit by a dim lamp. To the right of him were a set of steps that led down into darkness.

"Members only, mate," said the bloke. "It's sixty quid for membership and another thirty for entry, but after that you can come back as many times as you like during the week. Week after that, it's another thirty quid. Plus you gotta sign the register and show your membership card every time."

"The prophet Ezekiel said the women would kneel

on the steps of the Temple in Jerusalem, wailing and crying in lament for my death," said Jimmy. "By that time I was known as Tammuz and the crops would not grow if the women did not water the earth with their tears."

The bloke blinked five times rapidly and his eyes took on a glazed look. "Fair enough, it's down them steps just to the right there. Mind how you go cos it's a bit dark."

At the bottom of the steps was a narrow space lit by a dim red lightbulb. The walls were painted black and the floors were sticky with gum and other substances. There was a thick smell of stale sweat and old cigarette smoke in the air.

In the wall opposite was an opening covered by a black velvet curtain. Jimmy scanned the narrow space. In the dim gloom of the red bulb he saw a fat Semitic guy with tight curly hair, leaning up against the wall in the far corner. Kneeling in front of him was a slim, grey haired man who was sucking his long, fat cock.

Every now and again the guy would raise his hand and slap the grey haired man across the cheek, or grab his hair and force his head forwards so he swallowed the whole of the cock. The Semitic guy looked up and grinned at Jimmy.

Jimmy did not respond. He stepped forward and drew the black velvet curtain aside.

CHAPTER THIRTY-FIVE

JIMMY PASSED THROUGH into a small, shabby cinema. To his immediate right were about six rows of raked seats with two further rows of seats in front of them. The seats were worn and threadbare and the screen at the front was grubby and smeared with dirt.

The floor was even stickier and the smell of sweat and cigarette smoke was stronger. There were about ten men in the cinema, mostly sitting by themselves, but a few sat next to each other. One of the men had his hands down another's trousers.

On the screen, a large black woman was tied to a stained mattress. Two white men, in loin cloths and Ku Klux Klan hoods, stood over her. The woman was screaming at the men, calling them racist bastards. One of the men left and returned with an industrial sander that he applied to her nipple.

The woman bellowed in pain and anguish. The hand held camera moved closer, blood and viscera spattered the lens.

So this was the type of establishment Isimud was running. A private club screening torture flicks— authentic ones by the look of things. It made sense when Jimmy thought about it. It was exactly the place to recruit new victims. There was no sign of the man himself though.

Jimmy walked down the aisle to the front row. He didn't much care for the film. The robe had led him here, so Isimud must be nearby. A man got up from the front row and walked to the far corner of the cinema, right next to the screen. He touched the wall and a door appeared. As he went through the door, the man turned and caught Jimmy's eye. Jimmy only saw his face for the briefest moment, but he could swear it was the Turkish mini cab driver who'd picked Sam and him up on Bethnal Green Road.

Had the man been waiting for them? Was he in league with Isimud? For a second Jimmy had the sense of some giant cosmic mechanism moving behind the scenes of his recent life. Putting all the pieces into place to bring him to this very point. It was as though he'd had no choice about the direction of his life from the moment Ashkan clicked on the footage in the lock up.

Jimmy's plan was to blend in, get a feel of the place and not call too much attention to himself. The plan went out of the window the minute Jimmy sat down. His robe began to glow brighter than anything in the dim space, including the screen. Images from the footage began to tear free from the robe and launch themselves at the screen.

Jimmy looked up at the picture, which was glowing with twice its previous brightness. He saw the familiar cellar and there on the central operating table was Melissa. For a moment he was sure that she looked right out at him. Her expression seemed to acknowledge him and her eyes seemed to say 'not much longer now my love.' On the tables either side of her, Jimmy was horrified to see Ashkan and Sam.

The other patrons sat forward in their seats with a tense expectancy. There was a palpable sense that they were about to see something special. The type of unique entertainment they longed to find in this sort of establishment. The type that kept them coming back, day after day, in the hope it would appear. And now here it was, every bit as depraved and transgressive as they'd ever hoped.

Jimmy turned away from the screen and concentrated on the audience. He saw twisted hunger etched into their faces as they leered at the screen. Their mouths dropped open, their eyes widened with astonishment and disbelief. This was like nothing they'd ever seen before.

Jimmy watched as each of them was pushed to the limits of their endurance. Some shook their heads violently, others dropped their head in their hands. One man punched and kicked the seat in front of him in indignation. Many burst into tears. One by one they were beginning to discover that they were not so jaded or desensitised as they believed.

Finally someone stood up in disgust, swore at the screen and made to leave. Four other people got up to join him. The screen flared and the pictures on it bulged, growing in size until the edges appeared to tear and fray, becoming thin tendrils of light that spilled into the room as though probing it. Jimmy could no longer look away. Nor could anyone else in the cinema.

Whatever barriers, mental or emotional, that existed between the world of the screen and the world of the cinema, they had just been torn down. From the corner of his eyes, Jimmy saw a crowd of the blurred, shadowy Anunnaki slip from the edges of the screen and force their way into the cinema.

Jimmy couldn't look directly at the Anunnaki. Something in their physical make up forced the eye away. It was too painful to try and focus on them. He could feel their presence all around him but he couldn't take in their proper shape or form. They were just blurry shadows in his peripheral vision.

Jimmy wasn't sure if the other men could see the Anunnaki, but they certainly made their presence felt. Every sick and sadistic act those men had ever watched or gotten off on, was now visited on their own bodies. Whatever demons they were trying to exorcise in dim, furtive rooms like this one, were now coming back to claim them with a vengeance.

The four men outside the cinema, who Jimmy had met on his way in, were dragged in to join the slaughter. There didn't appear to be any sadism in the atrocities the Anunnaki committed, it was almost as if they were acting with a patient and methodical kindness. Purging the flesh of the men and the desires that had caused them such mental and spiritual pain.

The Anunnaki showed no sense of satisfaction when the slaughter had run its course. They simply remained still and resonated a calm melancholy.

Jimmy wasn't sure if the robe afforded him some sort of emotional protection, but he wasn't appalled or repulsed by the massacre he'd just witnessed. All he felt was the same calm sadness the Anunnaki were giving off.

It wasn't until someone startled him by clearing their throat, that Jimmy felt anything of note. He turned and saw a short Arabic man with thinning black hair and an immaculate white suit standing behind him.

Jimmy caught his breath. He recognised the man instantly, from his vision.

"Mr Isimud."

"So this is the famed Tailor's handiwork. It's even better than I dreamed. Such talent that man has, I'm almost breathless. You wouldn't mind just giving me a quick twirl would you? So I can get the full effect."

Jimmy did not oblige. He was too stunned. This was not what he was expecting. Mr Isimud looked disappointed.

"No?' he said. "Very well, if that's the way you're going to be, and after I waited so long as well. I was beginning to think you wouldn't make it."

"You're not the first person to say that to me today."

"So you make a habit of keeping people waiting do you? Or are you just a little slow off the mark? Never mind, don't answer that. I just hope you've been looking forward to this meeting as much as I have."

CHAPTER THIRTY-SIX

THE ISIMUD THAT stood before Jimmy, was not the man he'd seen in his vision. He was relaxed genial, and quite unbelievably charismatic. Like the Tailor he had the air of a man who does one thing so well that it brings him a great deal of power and influence, and nothing is more charismatic than that.

He also seemed to be filled with genuine anticipation. He was practically rubbing his hands together. This unnerved Jimmy more than anything. Something sinister lurked behind his anticipation, something more frightening than the maliciousness that played about his smile.

""Sometime towards the middle of the year 623 BC," Isimud continued. "Sin-shar-ishkun, one of the last Assyrian kings, led a large army into Babylonia to crush the rebel Babylonian forces led by King Nabopolassar. To begin with, the battle went in the Assyrian's favour and Nabopolassar's forces were routed. Then Sin-shar-ishkun's chariot followed his troops right up to the battle's front, where he met with Nabopolassar's equally impressive chariot.

"The two military rulers stood within feet of each other. Close enough to look one another in the eye. It is said there is an intimacy in combat unlike any other. Men who face each other in battle, whether generals commanding armies or foot soldiers fighting hand to hand, can look into each other's souls and know things about one another that no one else will. In that moment Sin-shar-ishkun saw his eventual ruin and Nabopolassar saw hard won victory. The Babylonian rallied his troops and fought to an eventual stalemate.

"Eight years later, Nabopolassar, in alliance with King Cyaxares, took the Assyrian city of Nineveh, killing Sin-shar-ishkun in the process. Soon after the whole Assyrian empire fell and Mesopotamia itself went into a slow decline. All of this foretold in a single glance between the heads of two formidable armies."

Mr Isimud looked Jimmy slowly up and down. "So tell me, dear boy" he said. "What do you see when you look into my eyes?"

Jimmy met Mr Isimud's gaze. He knew that Isimud was toying with him and it was exactly what he wanted Jimmy to do, but Jimmy wanted to show Isimud he was undaunted by the man's games.

"I've come back for Melissa," Jimmy said, trying to sound forceful.

Mr Isimud looked bemused. "Come back? I didn't realise you'd been here before."

"No, that's that not what I . . . that's beside the point, I've come for her and I'm going to set her free, like she wants."

"Set her free? You think that's what she wants?"

"Yes, to be free of you, free of this suffering."

"Why would she want to be free of it, when she's never been closer?"

"Closer? Closer to what?"

"My dear chap, why do think she's so prominent in my story?"

"Because you captured her, and . . . and tortured her."

"Because I captured her. Is that what you think? Then answer me this. If I really had captured her, how was she able to sneak away and spend time with you and your associate? Do you think I gave her a day pass, or time off for good behaviour?"

"No, but she was able to manifest because she's a character in the story, not a victim."

"Very good, you're not so clueless as I was beginning to fear. So let us consider this for a moment, how many characters do you know that were captured by their story? How many protagonists want to escape the tale they're in?"

"I don't know, maybe it depends on the story."

"Perhaps it does, but if Melissa truly wanted to escape, why do you think she sought me out in the first place? Why did she go to all the trouble of hunting me down, especially when, as you know, I'm not an easy man to find?"

"You tell me."

"And when she did finally find me, why do you think she begged me to be a part of the story?"

"Because you misled her, you lied to her and tricked her. Now she's trapped in the footage and forced to relive her death every time someone watches it."

"Oh dear, what a total failure of imagination you're showing. You stand here, draped in this miraculous creation, and all you can think, when you see its star player in all her glory, is that she's reliving her own death."

"That's how it looks to me."

"That's because you're not paying attention."

"Then what is happening?"

"At last, a sensible question. Melissa is living through the death and dismemberment of every person who ever died at the hands of this tale. She is slowly enduring six millennia of suffering."

Mr Isimud's eyes were alight with an almost messianic glee when he said this. Jimmy had seen a few of the murders the story had perpetrated. He couldn't imagine what it would be like to live through every one of them, one after the other, without any break from the endless violation, pain and degradation, for six thousand years. Jimmy couldn't think of a worse possible fate. He had to get Melissa out of this.

"And you're trying to tell me she begged for that?" he said. "Why would anyone beg for that?"

"Why wouldn't they? What does every human being dream of? Why do they tell themselves bedtime stories about heavenly sky fathers who love them simply because they exist? What do they hope to gain by currying favour with this celestial daddy?"

"To go to Heaven?"

"No, to live forever. Melissa doesn't want to be free. What she really wants, as you know full well, is to be immortal."

"What kind of immortality is that, being killed over and over again?"

"Is that what you think the Anunnaki are doing?"

"Having seen them in action a few times, I'd have to say yes, that's exactly what I think they're doing. I know they hate human flesh, because they think it's some kind of prison for God, but it's quite plain to see that they're killing her."

"No they're not. They're releasing her inner divinity. To live is to suffer, you see. Suffering is the true alchemist's crucible. It burns off all our impurities and reveals the God at the centre of our being. It transmutes our leaden lives into the gold of Godhood. Why do you think God descended into the prime material of His creation? So it would draw out all His impurities. This is why there is so much evil in the world. People ask how God could allow that without ever realising this is the purpose of the world."

"To get rid of God's evil?"

"Exactly, and as God descended, so the Anunnaki fell from grace and came to earth to enact His will."

"By doing evil?"

"No, by purging evil through suffering, and freeing the divine that lies at the centre of all life. The more suffering you endure, the purer you become. The purer you become, the stronger you are, stronger and closer to immortality."

"But what's in this for you? Why make Melissa immortal? What do you hope to gain out of this?"

"I am but an instrument of God's will. The whole of creation is merely God's story. 'In the beginning was the word . . . ' and who was the word with? Why God. That's because God is the ultimate story teller. We are all part of His story, but all stories are inevitably autobiographical and that is why God is trapped in His own story. We are all God, perceiving himself individually as the characters of His story. My story is the antidote."

"An antidote that can kill you."

"But of course, every antidote is a form of poison."

"So you made Melissa a character in your story so she could escape God's story?"

"That's what it's there for."

"She's not the first then?"

"She's the one who's come closest to transcending."

"Do you have any idea how much of a megalomaniac you sound?"

"Oh dear, so we've resorted to name calling now have we? It's a feature of the unremarkable mind that when it's faced with something it can't understand, it casts aspersion."

"'Unremarkable mind'—now who's name calling? I just wondered if you'd ever stopped to listen to yourself."

"If you're a gifted enough story teller, the whole universe will eventually stop to listen to you. That's the nature of a great story, that's the real power of words. Let me give you a demonstration."

Isimud turned to the screen where the footage was still playing. He pointed at it and said: "This is the door to my realm." The screen began to stretch and change shape as its edges reformed themselves.

"It leads to my land in the story-sphere," said Isimud. "I'm breaking the fourth wall, opening the door and bringing the story out to engulf us."

As Isimud spoke his words had a palpable effect on the reality around Jimmy. The words were like fish, swimming through the actuality surrounding them, sending out ripples as they went. Jimmy couldn't see the words but he could feel how powerful they were. They were doing Isimud's bidding, tugging at the realm of the story, pulling it through the rapidly growing screen into this world. It was like a bag of fluid being drawn through a window, it bulged and then it burst, flooding the cinema with its existence.

CHAPTER THIRTY-SEVEN

JIMMY WAS NO longer in the cinema, or anywhere in London.

He was in a giant underground space that seemed to stretch for miles in every direction. In places it looked like a cellar or a basement, in others a catacomb or a vault. In every area of the space there were people tied to operating tables, stone slabs and sacrificial altars with blurry Anunnaki buzzing round them, destroying and tormenting their flesh.

Jimmy was looking at the whole landscape of a murderous story that had no end. It was a limitless cartography of pain, showing every victim the story had ever taken, all suffering side by side. The atmosphere was like that of a charnel house, on a scale that Jimmy's mind just couldn't process. The air was so thick with human agony you could choke on it. Jimmy pulled the robe up around himself like a small child who pulls the blankets over his face, in the dead of night.

The hem of the robe had joined itself to the fabric of the story. There was no difference now between the material Jimmy was wearing and the world around him. It looked as if the stone slabs of the floor had risen up, to become a loose flowing textile, and draped themselves around Jimmy. It didn't impede his movement in any way and fitted him just as comfortably. Its shape and form remained the same, but its texture changed whenever he moved, to reflect wherever he was standing.

Jimmy closed his eyes, trying to block out all the sights and sounds, the millennia of anguish and suffering that surrounded him. Stay calm he told himself. Don't let it get to you. That's what this whole story was designed to do, push you beyond your limits. Just focus on your goals and objectives. Remember what you came here to do.

The Tailor had been very clear about his objectives. Jimmy had to administer the final cut and provide an ending for the story all around him. A fit and proper ending, one that tied up every loose end. As he'd told the Tailor though, he wasn't great with conclusive endings, he wasn't great with any kind of endings, they weren't his forte. If he was honest he could never really think of a way to wrap everything up in a story, that's why he liked to keep his stories open ended.

The story, where he now found himself, was dangerous principally because it was open ended. If he didn't find the right ending Melissa would never be free of it, would never get what she wanted.

She was counting on Jimmy to provide the final cut and free her. Could she have chosen a worse person? The Tailor had advised him to find whatever it was that stopped him from ending things. Jimmy hated endings, they brought only pain and loss. Jennie's death was the perfect example. That had been a sudden and irrevocable ending, with no doubts or hope of continuation. There was nothing ambiguous about it. One moment Jennie was in his life, the next she was gone, along with any chance of a future together.

Jimmy hated that, it wasn't fair. He would never do something like that to a character he'd created. Real life had done it to him and he knew how much it hurt. He turned to fiction to find the very opposite, the possibility of continuation, to hang on to things indefinitely. That's why he hung on to the pain he felt at losing Jennie, just like Suzy had said. He couldn't let it go, it was all he had to remember Jennie by. If he let go of the pain he'd have to admit that their life together really had ended and there was no way of making things up to her.

But now he was being forced to let it go, or he'd fail his mission and then neither he nor Melissa would be saved and he'd lose everything. He was weighing one loss against another, it was worse than a nightmare.

Jimmy felt the panic threaten to drown out his thoughts, as though someone had opened a cage of shrieking baboons at the back of his mind. He took a deep breath. It wasn't fair, it wasn't right, but he'd chosen to do this. No one was coming to save him. He had to face this all alone and redeem himself.

Jimmy opened his eyes and saw Mr Isimud standing next to the operating table where Melissa was strapped. Even though he was standing in the pits of a fictional Hell, Jimmy still felt a cool weight of emotion in his gut. When he looked at Melissa he couldn't stop the longing or the protective feelings. She offered him the means to redeem himself, and maybe that was all the saving he really needed.

"Well," said Mr Isimud. "It's the final chapter of

your story. Will it be the final chapter of Melissa's? I have to say I'm intrigued. You don't cut an impressive figure in the least, in spite of the immaculate cut of your clothes, but no one has ever made it to this place before. I'm excited to see how this ends."

"All you need to know is that it's going to end," said Jimmy.

"Given the six thousand year precedent, I rather doubt that."

Jimmy started to circle Isimud slowly, trying not to look at Melissa, his feelings for her were too raw. He was trying to get a sense of his surroundings, to see if there was anything he could use as a weapon and whether Isimud had any obvious weaknesses. Isimud observed him with a cool and amused detachment. Jimmy felt like a gazelle stalking a lion.

Jimmy got about ten steps away and found he couldn't go any farther. The robe simply wouldn't let him. It held him to the floor and wouldn't move any farther in that direction.

"I'm afraid those parts of the story are off limits to you at the moment," said Isimud. "You're only clothed in its latest incarnation. If you want to take off your robe, I'd be happy to take you for a tour though. You'd be astonished what happens to a story after six millennia of abducting and murdering everyone who encounters it."

Isimud had a predatory smile as he spoke, like a cat inviting a bird to come and play with its claws. He was toying with Jimmy, but he was also showing his hand. Isimud obviously wanted Jimmy to remove the robe, so that was the last thing he ought to do.

If the robe gave him an advantage he should

capitalise on that, but how? This whole place was the 'word made flesh' or, to be more precise, the 'word made flesh-ripping-monstrosity.' Isimud had used words to alter the footage and take Jimmy here. Maybe Jimmy could do the same.

"Thanks for the offer," Jimmy said. "But I think I'll pass. This robe is my armour, it's impregnable and it covers every inch of me, keeping me from harm."

As soon as he said this Jimmy could feel his words altering the intrinsic nature of the reality around him. What he said had a presence outside of the simple sound of his voice and the meaning others took from it. His words gathered up the robe from the floor and wrapped it around him. It changed from a flowing robe to a living shell that coated him from head to toe. It moved in perfect synch with his body but its outer layer was impregnable.

As he was coated in the story itself, Jimmy was all but invisible, especially if he stood still. If he moved he could only be detected by a slight ripple. Jimmy looked himself over and saw a tiny ragged hole in his armour, on the back of his right heel. The Tailor said the robe was unfinished due to the nature of its material. Naturally, being a story, it would leave him an Achilles heel.

Isimud's eyes widened with genuine admiration and he smiled, for perhaps the first time, with sincerity.

"Oh well done," Isimud said. "I am impressed. You might just be a worthy opponent after all."

Jimmy's chest swelled at the praise, in spite of his hatred and fear of Isimud. He was like a schoolboy who's been praised by the headmaster. Something at the back of his mind told him to be careful though. Isimud may be impressed, but he was still trying to play Jimmy. He was glad the armour hid his expression.

The armour might have been a clever move, but it was still a defensive one. Jimmy needed to go on the offensive. He needed something with which to make the final cut. He was using words and their power in a realm of story, just as Isimud was, but Isimud could still wield the Anunnaki in a way that Jimmy couldn't. So that's what Jimmy needed to do.

Jimmy strode towards one of the Anunnaki. He couldn't look at it directly, so he had to keep it in his peripheral vision as he reached out a hand to it. The Anunnaki bristled. Contact with flesh, even flesh clothed in story, was repugnant to it. Jimmy persisted.

"This Anunnaki is bound to me," he said. "I wear the story that it inhabits and it must follow all that I say. It is my weapon, a fearsome blade that can slice through anything in this realm or any other."

Jimmy could see the Anunnaki desperately wanted to resist, but his words went to work on it. It began to flicker and lose its current form, reshaping itself into a blurry, obsidian broadsword in Jimmy's hands. The hilt of the sword crackled against Jimmy's palms, shot through with a deadly electrical charge.

Mr Isimud applauded with slow deliberation, smiling sardonically. "Excellently played," he said. "The white knight is armed, but can he deliver the coup de grâce?"

Jimmy lifted his new blade. He could feel it crackle and buzz all the way down his arms and across his shoulders. It felt like an extension of his body, one that added grace and deadly precision to his movements. He needed to put an end to this story. He had to silence the voice that had given it form and substance. The teller of this tale must die.

Jimmy swung the sword at Isimud's throat. It seemed to pull his arm along with it, adding strength and momentum to the movement of the action. Something was wrong though. Jimmy locked his wrists and arms and the edge of the sword stopped just short of Isimud's jugular.

"So you don't have it in you after all," said Isimud. "All those deaths you've written and filmed and yet you're not actually capable of committing the act yourself."

Isimud was taunting him, but he was wrong. Jimmy was sunk deep in murder now. He'd crossed so many lines the act itself was but a short step to him. It was the look in Isimud's eyes that stayed his hand. For the briefest of moments Jimmy had seen bitter disappointment in them.

Isimud had been right about the intimacy between men who face each other in combat. It went deeper than he'd realised. In that brief flicker of disappointment, Jimmy saw a man made utterly despondent by the gilded prison of immortality.

Working in film and television, Jimmy had spent a lot of time around famous people, and he'd come to learn one thing about them, not one of them was satisfied with their status. For many of them, fame had taken a lot of hard work and sacrifice and, when it came, they found it wasn't the least bit worth it. Peter Cook had once said 'searching for happiness in fame is like looking for nutrition at the centre of a doughnut.' Worthless or not, fame was all they had to show for their efforts, so they clung to it, like the stiffening fingers of a corpse clinging to the poisoned chalice that took its life.

Jimmy saw the same response in Mr Isimud when it came to his immortality. He hadn't taken on Melissa, or the other characters, because he saw himself as an instrument of God. For all his heretical beliefs, he was flirting with his own ruin, putting himself in a situation where it could all be taken away from him, because secretly he knew it was wrong, that the balance must be restored and being immortal was nothing like he hoped it would be.

Jimmy also realised what had really scared him when he looked into Isimud's eyes. Behind the anticipation and the maliciousness, he had seen a dull and stultifying numbness. That must be the worst thing about being immortal, never having to worry about getting old or dying. Like his story, Isimud's life lacked an ending, and that took away all of its meaning.

That's what he was in search of now, that's why he'd invited Jimmy into the story to toy with him. He was trying to put some meaning back into his life. Like the pampered urbanites, who look to horror to give them back that primal thrill of living with the imminent threat of death, of facing the fight or flight situations of their ancestors. He wanted to feel alive again.

All he seemed to feel, when Jimmy was about to behead him, was disappointment. This told Jimmy one thing; killing Isimud would not bring an end to the story. Shakespeare was long dead, so were Dickens and

Austen, but their stories had more life than ever. You don't end a tale by killing the person who told it. This wouldn't end the story. Isimud would just come back to life, no matter how many times he was killed.

The Tailor told Jimmy there were many ways to finish a story, but only one way to truly end it. Every other attempt was a misstep, a distraction and would not lead to the tale's true ending. Killing Isimud was a misstep, and would not lead to this story's proper ending.

Jimmy let the sword fall, but held Isimud's gaze. Isimud raised a mocking eyebrow. There was something he was missing. What was it Isimud had said about his story? That it was the antidote to God's story. Creation was God's story and God was trapped in it, because He could only perceive Himself as the characters within that story. This was a core belief of Isimud's heresy, but it might also be the key to Jimmy's success. If we are all really one God, trapped in the story of creation, unable to see ourselves as anything other than individual characters, then that would mean . . .

Jimmy turned away from Isimud and walked to Melissa. She looked up at him with expectant longing and an anticipation even greater than Isimud's.

Jimmy raised his sword again and brought it down on her bonds, freeing her from the table. She sat up, massaging her wrists. Her breathing was quick and shallow, sweat broke on her chest and forehead and a vein throbbed in her neck as she watched him. Jimmy placed a hand on his chest, where the armour was thickest.

"This is no longer my armour," he said. "It is a robe once again."

Jimmy took off the robe, transferring the sword from hand to hand as he did. Then he draped the robe around Melissa's shoulders.

"This is your story," he said. "It belongs to you now. It is all about you and only you. You are Inanna, Persephone, Eurydice, Izanami-no-Mikoto and every mythic character that has ever ventured to Hell and sought to return."

Melissa's chest swelled with excitement. Her eyes shone with mounting hope, like the sun climbing the horizon. Jimmy put his hand on Melissa's shoulder and placed the tip of the sword against her stomach.

"Do it," said Melissa, guessing at Jimmy's intentions.

"No!" shouted Isimud, his voice alive with something he had all but forgotten: fear, genuine fear for his survival. This was more than the frisson that comes from flirting with danger, Isimud was facing his complete destruction. "Stop that, stop it now, I command you." But his words no longer had any power.

In that split second both Melissa and Isimud understood what Jimmy had realised. You don't end a story by killing the author. You end it by killing the characters. Without the characters there is no story. They are the divine element of every tale. They are God waiting to be released.

Now that he wasn't wearing the robe, the sword was fighting to return to its original form. Jimmy gripped the hilt tightly, willing the Anunnaki to hold its shape, and drove the blade into Melissa's midriff.

There was a wet rending sound as the blade tore through her stomach wall and punctured her intestines. Jimmy gagged at the thick smell of blood and intestinal gases. It flooded his nose and coated the back of his throat.

Melissa let out a strangled cry, half scream half sob, angry and dismayed by the intensity of the pain. When Jimmy had watched her die before, she had been so serene, so unflinching in her acceptance of the violence and mutilation. She showed none of that composure now.

This death was different. It was final.

For the first time in his career, Jimmy had found a way to end a story and not just abandon it.

CHAPTER THIRTY-EIGHT

MELISSA'S BODY WENT into convulsions. Her jaw hung open and started to spasm. Blood leaked from the corner of her mouth and an agonising moan escaped from her throat. Her torso shook as her body went into shock and a torrent of blood spilled from her wound, pouring over the edge of the table and onto Jimmy's feet.

Jimmy gripped Melissa's shoulder as the blade squirmed in his hands, trying to shrug off the form it was currently holding. It looked like an image on a TV with bad reception, crackling in and out of shape. This ruptured Melissa's organs and caused her to cough up more blood.

Melissa threw her head back and stopped shaking, her breath barely perceptible. The robe around her shoulders started to liquefy and soak into her pores. Her skin was absorbing it, becoming one with the Tailor's handiwork.

As the robe merged with her flesh, and then her bones, Melissa's body began to change. Her breasts disappeared and chest hairs sprouted in their place. Her legs and body grew and her shoulders broadened. Stubble spread across her chin and her hair restyled itself, twisting into a man-bun. Jimmy found he was looking into the eyes of his friend Sam.

Sam glanced down at the writhing sword embedded in his middle, then looked up at Jimmy with dismay. A hundred unspoken things passed between them in that look. Jimmy tried to find the words to express them, but his throat closed up and his lips moved in silence. His words were drowned by the sudden fear that, once again, he might have tried to save the wrong person, allowing someone he loved to die.

As if he sensed this, Sam shuddered and started to shrink. The stubble retreated back into his face and his chest hairs were replaced by breasts. His hair changed colour and fell about his shoulders, becoming wet and rain soaked. Jimmy was now confronted by Jennie. She was naked, but other than that, she was just as he last saw her, at the side of that country lane.

She looked up at him and dissolved into floods of tears. She didn't have to look down at the sword to see what Jimmy had done to her. She simply cried for the fact that this was their one last chance to be together and Jimmy had killed her all over again, but worse this time, much, much worse.

Jimmy began to cry and the tears finally freed up his words. "I'm sorry," he said, speaking to Sam as much as to Jennie. "It's my fault you died. I should have been there. I should have come back. I know that now. If I could just take your place, if it could only be me instead of either of you . . . "

And there it was. He hadn't let go of the pain, even if he had ended the story. He not only wanted to hang on to his own pain, he wanted to take Sam and Jennie's pain away from them and make it his own.

He could hang on to his pain, but he couldn't keep

hold of the sword. It shrugged off Jimmy's grip and shot straight through Jennie, tearing a gaping hole in her back. It re-formed itself into an Anunnaki at the head of the operating table.

Jennie's eyes rolled up into her head and she fell backwards against the table. Her body deflated as she fell, losing all its form and substance, until she landed on the table top as nothing more than an empty robe. The robe slipped off the surface of the table, hit the floor and melted away to nothing. The stone slabs mopped it up like sponges.

"What have you done?" screamed Isimud. "You idiot! You have no idea. You have no idea what you've done!"

Jimmy turned to face him. The little man was incandescent with rage. His nostrils flared, the veins throbbed in his bright red temples and his eyes bulged with anger. The force of it was so great that Jimmy took several steps backwards, as though blown by a strong gale. His hip crashed into the corner of a table, his heel got caught on the leg and he stumbled backwards.

The table was empty. Jimmy looked around the story space and saw that all the tables were now empty, as were the slabs and the sacrificial altars. All the victims were gone. The mood and the atmosphere of the whole place had changed, too. The despondent pall of agony and suffering that hung over everything had dissipated.

It was replaced by a sense of impending menace, as the many Anunnaki looked around them and saw no one to maim and torture but Jimmy and Mr Isimud. They left their posts and began to advance on the pair of them.

CHAPTER THIRTY-NINE

JIMMY DARTED BEHIND one table and then another, trying to get as far away from the Anunnaki as possible, but nothing stopped their advance. Eventually he pushed himself up against a wall and sunk down into a squat with his arms over his head, naked and vulnerable, wearing only his boxers.

The Anunnaki pushed right past him as though he wasn't there. They were interested only in Mr Isimud. They fell on him in a blurred and shadowy mass. Jimmy pulled himself up and sat on the edge of a table.

It was impossible to look directly at the massive scrum of Anunnaki surrounding Isimud. To try and take it in hurt not only Jimmy's eyes, but also his soul.

Jimmy turned away and tried to block out first Isimud's screams and then the sounds of rending and tearing. The Anunnaki began to separate into smaller mobs each carrying a different Isimud, kicking and thrashing in their grip.

Jimmy's eyes couldn't process the mass huddle of Anunnaki that had fallen on Isimud. The sight of so many blurred and shadowy figures caused them to throb. He could only focus on the occasional glimpse of Isimud himself, lying on the floor screaming and lashing out at his captors. The Anunnaki appeared to be peeling and tearing identical versions of Isimud from the captive original lying on the floor. Almost as if they were peeling sheets from a daily calendar.

Jimmy didn't understand what he was seeing at first. Then it dawned on him; Isimud was being separated into all the lifetimes he would have lived over the course of the six millennia he'd been alive.

The Anunnaki carried each Isimud to a table or a slab and went to work on him as only they were capable. Visiting upon him the same frenzied damage and depravation they'd visited upon all his story's victims.

A darkness was encroaching on the space and whole sections were simply winking out of existence. As soon as one group of Anunnaki finished dispatching their version of Mr Isimud, the space they were inhabiting shut down and vanished completely.

As six thousand years' worth of Isimud's dying screams slowly faded, the whole realm receded into a tiny area of floor and one single operating table where Jimmy was perched, his knees drawn up under his chin.

CHAPTER FORTY

JIMMY COULDN'T STOP shivering, not just from the chill air, but from everything he'd been through. He wanted to cry, but was afraid he'd lose himself to hysteria. His chest wheezed as his asthma threatened to return.

He knew at some point he'd have to climb down from the table and explore the tiny space. He wouldn't find a way out otherwise, if there was a way out. At the moment though, all he wanted to do was hug his knees and rock gently back and forth.

The darkness that surrounded the tiny area was thick, black and seemingly absolute. Beyond it were beings more dangerous than Jimmy could comprehend.

He had no idea what to do if he couldn't find a way out. He hadn't thought this far ahead. He never did. He wasn't a great finisher or completer, he needed Sam for that. He was an initiator. He launched into the things on impulse without a thought for where they might go or how they might end.

It all came down to endings yet again. It always did. It wasn't supposed to end like this though. Why hadn't he been saved as the Tailor promised?

As if in answer to his question, two Anunnaki

stepped out of the darkness. Jimmy bit his lip so hard he tasted blood. He pulled his knees up over his face and hugged his legs, rocking frantically. He expected the Anunnaki to strike any moment, but nothing happened.

After an agonising while he looked up and peered over his knees at them. The Anunnaki weren't paying Jimmy the slightest bit of attention. Their heads were bowed and they were examining the stone floor, searching for something. Without looking directly at them, Jimmy watched as they identified a spot and reached down into the floor.

The stone slabs seemed to change their composition as the Anunnaki reached into them, becoming more like loosely draped cloth. The Anunnaki lifted this cloth and, as they pulled it up, it began to resemble human skin.

The skin filled out, forming legs, arms, breasts and a head. The figure came to life in front of Jimmy. He nearly sobbed with relief when he saw who it was, her image blurred by the tears pouring from his eyes.

"Melissa, oh thank God . . . thank God. I thought I was never going to get out of here."

"You aren't," she said. "Not for a long, long time anyway."

Jimmy blinked the tears away and stared at Melissa with incomprehension. Why was she acting so cold?

"What do you mean?" he said. "I thought you'd come to help me, to get me out of here."

"Now why would I want to do that?"

"Because I came back for you, like you asked. I set you free."

"You rammed a bloody great sword into my guts."

"Only so I could end the story and get you out. So you could be free, like you wanted."

"Ah yes, what I wanted. I heard your little conversation with Isimud. Men, you're all so alike, always telling a woman what she wants, without actually listening to her. That's what made it so easy to play you off against each other."

"What do you mean?"

"Oh dear, the penny still hasn't dropped, has it? How easily I played you and Isimud. Both thinking you knew what was good for me and what I wanted. I did want to be free of the endless suffering, just as you said, but I didn't want to be rescued by some knight in armour. And I do want immortality, but not the type Isimud was offering. Who wants to endure so much suffering they get purified? What I really wanted was what Isimud had. I wanted the story and I wanted you to help me get it, which you did."

"I did?"

"Yes, you covered me with the robe remember, and you said the story was 'my story' and 'all about me,' just as I wanted you to. Mr Isimud was quite right when he said, all stories are autobiographical at heart, and now he's gone, the story really is 'all about me,' and that makes me the teller of the tale. I own the story, just as I always wanted. Now I really will be immortal, but on my own terms. Just as soon as I rebuild it."

The Anunnaki moved a little closer to Jimmy. He didn't like where this conversation was going. "What do you mean by 'rebuild it?'"

Melissa's brow wrinkled with annoyance. "You do

ask a lot of questions, do you know that? It's not one of your most attractive traits."

"I'm sorry."

"Oh God, don't apologise, that just makes you sound pathetic, and that would be out of character. You see, you are a character now, just as I was. You put on the robe and stepped into the story, you chose to become the character I asked you to be, Dumuzi the shepherd king."

"And I was Dumuzi. I came to Hell for you. I rescued you, just like Dumzi rescued Inanna."

"Oh my dear, sweet Jimmy," Melissa moved closer to him and stroked his cheek with the back of her hand. Her touch was soft and warm, and surprisingly comforting. It was the first sign of affection anyone had shown Jimmy in an age. He would have relished it, had the Anunnaki not closed in around him as well.

"Your aversion to endings was one of the reasons I chose you," Melissa said. "I knew you wouldn't read ahead and find out how the myth ended, but you really should have. Inanna isn't rescued by Dumuzi. The god Enki comes to her aid but, in order to leave the underworld, she has to find someone to take her place. Dumuzi didn't come and help Inanna when she asked him, just as you didn't come to Jennie's aid. So she had him seized by demons and dragged to Hell in her place."

The Anunnaki grabbed Jimmy's wrists and dragged him back till he was lying prone against the table with his hands above his head. Then they began to strap him in. There was a fierce tingle to their touch, like an electrical charge. There was no animosity in their actions, they acted with what seemed like calm benevolence.

"Wait," Jimmy said. "What are you doing?"

"Again with the questions, isn't it obvious? I'm rebuilding the story."

"What?"

"Oh please stop, you're embarrassing yourself. The other reason I chose you was because, like me, you can't let go of your pain. In fact, you're worse than I am, no amount of closure can stop you hanging on to it. You store up pain and never let it go. This story feeds on pain and grows because of it. Do you realise how perfect that makes you?"

"That's not how it works though. I made the final cut, I ended the story. You got what you wanted and I'm supposed to be saved. There are rules to every story, the Tailor told me."

"And I believe he also told you the best stories never follow these rules quite how you'd expect."

"But I'm supposed to be saved."

"And you will be saved, by living through the deaths of every victim this story has ever taken. It's the only salvation this story can offer you. It's also the only way to rebuild the story, one agonising death at a time, until it's back to its old monstrous size."

One of the Anunnaki produced a sacrificial knife. The other ran an appraising hand over Jimmy's chest, the crackling touch reminded Jimmy of how frail his body was. He'd seen them slice and peel skin like his. He'd watched as they tore and shredded flesh as tender as his own. He knew how fragile his bones would be in the sombre hands of the Anunnaki.

Jimmy had seen what six thousand years of torment is like and now it lay ahead of him, without any hope of a reprieve.

"Wait, this isn't fair," he said. "This isn't how the story's supposed to end."

Melissa placed a kiss on his forehead and put her lips to his ear. "Now don't be that way. I thought it would rather appeal to you. You see, this story is never supposed to end, even when it finishes. You carry it away with you, in your heart and mind, haunted relentlessly from the moment you reach the last line . . . "

POOR, OLD JIMMY, SO TRUSTING, SO DOOMED. AND NOW YOU'VE REACHED THE LAST LINE, GENTLE READER, THE STORY IS YOURS TO CARRY AWAY IN YOUR HEART AND MIND.
OR IS IT CARRYING YOU IN ITS HEART AND MIND? CAN YOU ESCAPE ITS RELENTLESS HAUNTING? IS THERE ANY ESCAPE?
I COULDN'T POSSIBLY TELL YOU, BUT IF YOU GRAB ALL THE OTHER BOOKS IN THE BARK BITES HORROR LINE YOU MIGHT JUST FIND OUT. TRUST YOUR UNCLE JASP ON THIS, YOU KNOW IT MAKES SENSE.
TUÑÓN BENZO

The Qu'rm Saddic Heresy
by Nicola Tanthus PhD,
Associate Professor, Camford University

The Qu'rm Saddic Heresy, also known as the 'Faith that Comes Before Man' and the 'Oldest Truth,' is one of those enigmatic by-roads travelled by scholars of antiquity, especially those interested in lost and ancient beliefs. As with other heretics such the Gnostics, the Bogomils and the Cathars, most of what we know about the heresy comes from its harshest critics. But whereas many works have come to light, in the case of Gnosticism, that allow the heretics to speak to us across the ages, no document has yet been discovered that belongs to this heretical set of beliefs. Though the ancient Greek scholar, Achaikos of Thebes, informs us its adherents claimed all religious beliefs stem from this heresy and are a mere corruption of the more profound truths it contains.

This belief is mirrored in the writing of Italian scholar and Catholic priest Marsilio Ficino, who proposed the doctrine of the *Prisca Theologia*, which asserts that a single true theology exists, one that underlies all world religions, and was given by God to man in antiquity. Ficino, the first modern translator of both the *Corpus Hermeticum* and the works of Plato, never directly referred to the Qu'rm Saddic heresy in his writing. However, later commentators on his work have inferred certain references to it. Given the precarious political situation that Ficino operated in, and given that he was a proponent of pagan philosophers in a highly Christian power structure, it is not surprising that he would not make any direct reference to a heresy that, if the rumours are to be believed, has been brutally suppressed since religion became organised and allied to the state.[1]

Ficino's brilliant, but ultimately doomed disciple Giovanni Pico Mirandola is also said to have made veiled allusions to the Qu'rm Saddic heresy in his much feted *900 Theses* and his *Oration on the Dignity of Man*.[2] There are some that have hinted that Mirandola's mysterious death by poison at the young age of 31 may have been linked to the heresy. That other most famous Renaissance philosopher: Giordano Bruno, was also rumored to be in possession of certain scrolls that pertained to the ancient heresy. Given that Bruno was subsequently burned at the stake for heresy himself in February 17th, 1600, some fringe historians have speculated as to the truth of these rumours.[3]

Ficino, Mirandola and Bruno were scholars who rescued ancient pagan philosophies and made them available to early Enlightenment audiences. By the time they were doing this, the Qu'rm Saddic Heresy was already considered impossibly old. One of the earliest references we have to the heresy comes from the Ebla Tablets, 1800 clay cuneiform tablets found in the Syrian city of Ebla. The tablets speak of an incident in the Mesopotamian city of Harran, one of the oldest human settlements and the site of perhaps the world's

---

1. Yates, Frances *Giardano Bruno and the Hermetic Tradition* (1964) pp 15
    ISBN-10: 041527849X
2. Ibid
3. Lachman, Gary *The Quest for Hermes Trismegistus* (2011) pp 210, ISBN-13: 978-0863157981

first university, or centre of learning. Harran was linked to Elba due to the marriage of an Harranian city ruler to the Eblanian princess Zugalum.[4] Even when the tablets were written, the incident was said to be ancient history. It concerns the expulsion of a school of heretics, from the university, who were said to be misleading the student body with their blasphemous teachings. This is the first time the heresy is referred to as the Qu'rm Saddic heresy, though no explanation is given as to where this name originates. The heretics in question were summarily stoned to death.

Although I stated earlier that no actual texts outlining the beliefs of the heretics have survived, Johannes Hennenbloch, the 17th century Swiss scholar, claimed that the mysterious Voynich Manuscript was in fact a copy of a text central to the heresy. Dating to the 15th century, the manuscript was purchased by the Holy Roman Emperor Rudolph from Dr. John Dee in 1586. Believed to have been written by Roger Bacon, the volume contains many pages of an indecipherable text accompanying strange botanical and zodiacal drawings. No one has ever been able to decipher the writings but Hennenbloch makes an interesting argument for them being part of a lost cannon of the Qu'rm Saddic heresy.[5]

Subtle allusions to the heresy have appeared in many occult writings down through the ages. Most notably in the works of Christian Rosenkreuz and other Rosicrucians, then later in the writings of the Theosophists Madame Blavatsky and Rudolph Steiner as well as the mystic G. I Gurdjieff. Perhaps the most

---

4. Moorey, Peter Roger Stuart , A Century of Biblical Archaeology (1991), pp 149, ISBN 978-0-664-25392-9.
5. To view the Voynich manuscript and decide for yourself go to http://beinecke.library.yale.edu/collections/highlights/voynich-manuscript

interesting development in the history of the heresy was its adoption by weird fiction writers in the early 20th Century.

Little is known about the life of Herbert W. Soames, other than that he lived in Schenectady, and published in the pulp magazines of the early 20th century, most notably between 1919 to 1931. Many of his most salubrious and sensational stories featured references to the heresy that, in spite of their many literary faults, suggest the author had a knowledge of the more esoteric strands of the Qu'rm Saddic beliefs. Titles such as *Murder in the Name of Monanom, Blood for the Byrflings* and *My Heart Beats Fast for the Heolfor* thrilled readers of such forgotten publications as *Racy Tales, The Red Book* and *All Male Stories*.

In contrast, L.P. Hartington was a Don of the University of Camford, who in 1940 published a slim collection of stories entitled *Late in the Day it Came to Pass*. The stories are very much in the vein of M. R. James, Walter De La Mere and Lord Dunsany. While they lack the power and artistry of those same writers, one or two of them are eerily effective, especially the haunting and morose *Why the Willows Weep for Me*. All but two of the eight stories in the small volume deal in one way or another with concepts that are central to the Qu'rm Saddic heresy.

Both authors are long out of print. Soames's work was never collected, and Hartington's had a limited print run. As a consequence, the stories never appear online and are seldom to be found in the back catalogues of booksellers. If you do come across a copy of *Late in the Day it Came to Pass*, or a pulp containing Soames's work, be warned, despite their scarcity and novelty, their literary merits do not match the exorbitant prices that are asked for them.

In spite of the Western occult revival that began in the 1960s, the Qu'rm Saddic heresy was almost completely ignored by esoteric writers in the latter half of the 20th century. I am reliably informed, however, that it has recently come back into favour as a fictional theme in the early part of the 21st century. I have not read the works of such writers as L.L. Smith, Jasper Bark or Simone Lastwick, whose work is said to touch upon the heresy, but I am reliably informed that there is little there to recommend them, other than a macabre ingenuity and a tiny amount of scholarship.

What is most astonishing about the Qu'rm Saddic heresy, is that a belief system that was said to be old when our most ancient records were made, should still exert a hold on the contemporary imagination. There is an allure that surrounds forbidden truths and a certain mystique about banned beliefs. A sense of longing pervades their study, a yearning for deeper answers and a better glimpse into the darker matters of the cosmos.

This is perhaps why they inspire such frightful fiction (in both senses of the word). It's also why the unwary and the foolhardy seek to learn more about them. There is something within human nature that can't help but question the perceived wisdom of its age. That's why there will always be heretics and heresy, and why we seek out dark truths that may best be left to antiquity.

Crystal Lake Publishing would like to thank the author for her kind permission to reproduce this work.

EXCERPTED FROM
RUN TO GROUND
BY
JASPER BARK

1:

THERE WAS SOMETHING wrong with the shed. Jim knew the moment he saw it.

It was an innocuous little building that sat against the far cemetery wall. Jim kept his tools there, along with his work clothes, the ride-on mower and anything else he needed for groundskeeping.

Yesterday, Cundle had requisitioned it for all his fancy equipment. Jim had moved most of the tools into the bungalow where he lived, on the outskirts of the cemetery. There were a few things he still needed to pick up, and he was curious to see what sort of mess Cundle had made of the place, with all his seismological apparatus.

The first thing Jim noticed, as he drew nearer, was the amount of flies buzzing around the shed. They hovered in a cloud and the noise they made was like a distant engine.

The door was open, creaking on its rusty hinges. There was a thick smell in the air that grew stronger the closer Jim got. It reminded Jim of his father's overalls when he worked at the abattoir.

Jim had no idea what Cundle was doing in the shed but it was time to put a stop to it. He didn't care how high up he was at the university, or how much of an

245

expert he was supposed to be, he was up to no good. Jim wasn't going to let him get away with it, not in his shed.

The cloying smell, and the drone of the flies, increased as Jim reached the door. He put his hand over his nose and mouth as he pulled the door open. A wave of flies swarmed out and Jim waved them away with his free hand.

The dim bulb that hung from the ceiling had been shattered and it took Jim a while to see through the gloom inside the shed. When his eyes had adjusted to the dim light, his brain took a while to process what he was seeing.

Every piece of equipment in the whole shed had been destroyed. The camp table Cundle brought had been knocked aside and bent out of shape. His laptops and seismological apparatus lay in pieces in the corners of the shed.

A stray electric cable, with its torn wires exposed, lay crackling in a pool of water. Except the liquid was too thick to be water, and it was the wrong colour. It was dark crimson and covered the entire floor of the shed. Its surface was beginning to congeal as Jim waded into the shed looking for Cundle. It began to seep into Jim's new trainers.

That's when Jim saw Cundle, and wished he hadn't.

Cundle lay face down with his knees pulled up underneath him. His back was arched. What remained of his head was thrown back and his posterior was in the air. His trousers were torn to shreds and Jim clearly saw the foot-thick column of compacted earth that appeared to have burst up through the boards of the floor and buried itself in Cundle's impossibly distended rectum.

Cundle's buttocks were pushed so far apart to accommodate the shaft of soil, that the flesh around his anus was torn and ruptured. The earth had forced itself so hard and so deep into Cundle's behind it seemed to have pushed every one of his internal organs out the opposite end.

Cundle's mouth had been thrown wide open by the expulsion. His jaw was not only dislocated but the bones had cracked and come apart entirely. The glistening pink tubes of Cundle's lower colon protruded from his torn and ragged lips, spilling out into the lake of blood and bile in front of him. Jim saw what he thought was a liver and a pair of lungs among the coils of dripping innards and the crawling flies.

This couldn't be happening. Jim's mind just couldn't make sense of the scene before him. Who could have done this? How was such a thing possible?

Only this morning Cundle had been fussing around the graves and bossing Jim about as though he was Cundle's lackey. Looking down his nose at Jim the whole time. Now he was reduced to this.

Jim felt a wave of revulsion, then a deep, terrible pity. He hadn't liked Cundle while he was alive. He'd found the man to be pompous and condescending. Jim's menial job left him beneath Cundle's consideration. All the same, he'd been a human being, capable of thought and compassion. He didn't deserve a fate like this.

Jim wondered what Cundle had been thinking in the final moments, as the fear gripped him and the agony of the violation became unbearable? Did he call out for his mother, or his children, if he had any? Did he long for the touch of an old flame, or just pray it would end quickly so the pain would finally stop?

It didn't make any sense. How had the ground just risen up and punched a hole through the floor like that? How had it impaled Cundle and filled him so full of earth that every one of his internal organs had been expelled? Things had been getting weird around the cemetery lately, but this was off the scale.

Jim felt his stomach turn over. Not from the sight of Cundle but from a new smell that invaded the shed. It was growing stronger by the second. He'd thought it was coming from Cundle, but it was too cloying and putrid. It reeked of decay and rotting matter, so rancid it was almost fertile. A shameful sort of fertility, like the mould that grows on dead things. The smell not only grew, it began to envelop him, as though it were alive—another presence in the shed with him.

The floor shook and something beneath the wooden boards rumbled, as though it were moving through the earth directly below the shed. It might even be the thing that had killed Cundle.

Jim's breathing got heavier and his skin went cold all over, even as the sweat broke out on the back of his neck. He realised he was in great danger, not just of death, but the same slow, hideous torture that Cundle would have suffered.

He had to leave the shed right now and put as much distance possible between himself and whatever was under it. Jim turned on his heel and fled into the cemetery.

2:

HE HAD TO get to Sloman's office. Sloman could call the police, or the fire brigade, or whomever it took to fix this. The cemetery was large, covering many acres, but Jim had worked there nearly six months now, so he knew the quickest route.

As he ran down the asphalt path Jim felt the ground beside it rumble. Whatever had been underneath the shed was now chasing him. It was in the earth right beneath him. Something was terribly wrong, things like this shouldn't happen. What had Cundle been doing in the shed to cause this to happen?

Jim's heart pumped and the blood sang in his ears, colours seemed brighter and his vision was sharper. Jim could pick out individual blades of grass and petals on a daisy.

His cousin, a head-case who'd done two tours in Iraq, once told him this happened under fire. In fight or flight situations, all your senses went into overdrive and you knew things without realising how.

Jim was experiencing that now. He couldn't tell how, but he knew whatever was pursuing him wasn't burrowing beneath the earth, it was becoming it. The ground was too smooth and undisturbed for it to be digging. Somehow it was possessing the soil, like a vengeful spirit, converting the earth to whatever it was, then releasing it as it moved alongside the path in pursuit of him.

Jim's pursuer overtook him and circled round in front, becoming the asphalt path in front of him. The asphalt up ahead rippled like it was suddenly gelatinous and the rumbling took on a harsher tone—the growl of a beast about to attack.

Jim turned and ran back up the path, tearing away from whatever was blocking his way. He spotted another path, branching off on his right, it would take him a little off course but he could still circle back and get to Sloman's office. His pursuer followed, keeping time with Jim, sometimes beside the path, sometimes behind him, rumbling loudly like a hound nipping at his heels.

Jim came to a fork in the path and headed right to Sloman's office. Whatever was pursuing him sped up and blocked his way again. Jim was forced to take the other fork. It's playing with me, he thought. Pushing me down the route it wants me to take.

Jim was panting and his lungs were beginning to burn. He wasn't in the best shape and the running was taking its toll. Halfway down the new path he saw the grave. He recognised it instantly. The gravestone was unique; Jim knew every inch of it intimately. The moment he saw it he knew why the thing in the ground had guided him here.

The ground in front of the gravestone had sunk into a deep depression, like a grassy pit. What made it look even odder was the way the turf all around it was folded in on itself. As though the grass was a balloon that had been deflated or the stretched and flabby skin of someone who's undergone rapid weight loss. It had looked very different several days ago.

3:

A Week Earlier . . .

CUNDLE RUBBED HIS bald patch, and sighed. He was a short bloke with a neatly trimmed beard and glasses. His belly hung over the front of his jeans, stretching the trendy T-shirt he wore.

"Any idea what's causing it?" said Sloman, who was tall and thin with a long face and a liking for tweed jackets, which made him look older than he was.

"I do have a theory," said Cundle. "But it's still hypothetical and not very conventional I'm afraid."

Sloman and Jim exchanged a look, Cundle had a habit of talking like he was giving a lecture. Cundle stepped forward and patted the hillock that had sprung up on the grave. The ground all around it was perfectly level, but the grave itself had developed a mini hill that was at least five feet high. Its shape was unusually bulbous and reminded Jim of the distended belly of a famine victim.

The hill had been growing slowly, like a bulge in the earth, for the past three months, getting noticeably larger by the week. The grave was one of three affected in this way, all of them growing large swollen mounds. Jim was very well acquainted with each of the graves and had originally brought the matter to Sloman's attention.

Sloman hadn't thought it important at first, but when the mounds began to swell up into little hills he'd gotten in touch with the cemetery's trustees and they'd found some money to get an expert to investigate. That's when Cundle had been called in. He was a professor at a nearby university.

"I think the graves are being affected by the moon," Cundle said. Jim rolled his eyes and Sloman shook his head to quiet him.

"We know that the moon affects the tides," Cundle continued. "But it's my belief that it has a similar effect on the outer layers of the earth's crust. Usually this effect takes place over such a long period of time we can hardly account for it, but occasionally there are anomalies such as this one. Phenomena that point to the extraordinary effect of the moon on the ground beneath our feet."

"Do you know how we can fix it then?" said Sloman. "Without taking a bulldozer to 'em."

"Oh no, you can't bulldoze these graves. This is a site of great scientific importance. I shall have to come back in a week's time when the moon's at its lowest ebb to do some more tests and then some weeks later when it's at its fullest. All tests will have to be conducted after midnight, so I'll need access to the cemetery then."

Sloman frowned, annoyed that Cundle wanted to study the problem, not fix it. "Jim'll let you in," he said. "He lives on the grounds and he's often up and prowling around at night. Isn't that right, Jim?"

Jim blushed at this. He put his hand in his pocket and adjusted his boxer shorts. A few crumbs of soil fell out and he shook them from his trouser leg without the others noticing.

4:

THE GRAVE HAD fallen in that morning, before Cundle arrived with his fancy equipment. He looked crestfallen when Jim showed him. He had no explanation for the dramatic collapse of the hillock, and didn't understand why it had sunk in on itself in a matter of hours.

Cundle acted as though his precious theory had collapsed along with the grave. He seemed to take comfort in the fact that there had been localised tremors in the area just before the collapse.

As Jim tore past the grave now, he noticed something new. At its foot was a long vertical slit in the earth, almost a gash, where the turf had been pulled apart. In the waning light of the early evening, he could just make out that the gash opened onto a small tunnel.

It took ten minutes to get to Sloman's office from the grave. Jim's legs shook, he knew he couldn't keep up the pace. He wondered for a minute if he shouldn't just lie down on the grave and get it over with. Then he thought of Cundle and what had been done to him and the fear of that spurred him on. Now that Jim had seen the grave, whatever was chasing him seemed content to hover two steps behind him. If he slowed to a walk, it would move closer and worry him, like a sheepdog herding a stray.

Sloman's office was by the main gates, a single storey building with a gabled roof that had once been the cemetery keeper's cottage. Now it served as a visitor's centre and workplace for Sloman. The largest room contained a little display about the history of the cemetery and a few shelves with 'local interest' books. In the back was Sloman's office, a small kitchen and a toilet.

It was usually locked at this hour. Jim fumbled the keys from his pocket as he jogged up. He noticed the main gates were chained and padlocked. Jim hadn't seen the big padlock before and he had no key for it. He had no idea who'd done it, but it changed all his plans. He'd hoped to get the hell out of the cemetery the minute he'd alerted Sloman. Now he'd have to make his way out of one of the side entrances. That meant facing whatever was out there again.

Jim's heart sank the minute he entered the largest room. Something was obviously not right. For a start there was the smell again. It was fainter, but it was definitely there, heavy with rot and a sickening ripeness.

The strip lights in the main room were flickering, but the office out back was in shadow. Jim had expected to hear Sloman at work, typing on his laptop or chatting on the phone. Instead the whole place was dead silent, too silent. The door to the office was slightly ajar. Jim couldn't see beyond it.

He felt like he was in a horror movie. He realised this was the moment when the audience would scream for him to get the hell out, to turn around, run or do anything other than go in that back office. It was one of the reasons he couldn't watch horror movies. He couldn't believe how stupid most of the characters were.

Yet here he was walking towards the office at the back like there was a horrible inevitability to it, as though he had no other choice but to do this. In real life, he thought, sometimes you don't.

Jim pushed open the door and stepped into the office. He let out a sob when he saw Sloman. He sounded like a little school girl. Suddenly he felt very detached from his body, as though he were far away from that office, watching it all from a safe distance.

He hadn't liked Cundle very much, but Sloman was a different matter. Sloman was a decent guy and he'd been good to Jim.

He shook his head and blinked the tears out of his eyes. He couldn't take in what had happened to Sloman, his brain couldn't process it. It was like trying to decipher an unknown language or work out an entirely new branch of mathematics, wholly beyond his comprehension.

Every bit of furniture was shattered. Sloman's laptop, his cable router and his radio lay in tiny pieces on the ground. The walls, floor and ceiling ran with blood and viscera. Thick, viscose droplets fell all about Jim.

The bones from Sloman's disassembled body were scattered around the room in strange geometric arrangements. Bits of cartilage and tendon still stuck to some. Jim couldn't grasp anymore than that, his mind wouldn't let him.

There was a slight tremor in the ground, causing

all of Sloman's bones to rattle. The same fetid odour rose in the office like a sudden increase in temperature. Jim started to back out when his foot kicked something that skittered out of the doorway. He turned to look and saw it was Sloman's hand, the only part of his body to remain intact. It had been severed at the wrist but Jim could still see his wedding ring.

The fingers of the hand were clutching something. Jim bent to get a better look and saw it was Sloman's phone. A tiny flutter of hope awoke in him. There might just be a way out of this, he could still call for help. Jim had not owned a phone, a laptop or a tablet since he came to the cemetery. It was one of the things he did to stay off the grid and avoid detection. He regretted that now. He desperately needed to connect to the outside world.

Jim pried the phone from the still warm fingers of the hand and tapped the screen to check for a signal. No bars were showing, but the screen was open on a text conversation. He swallowed hard. He was sure he recognised the number and it made him nauseous. The most recent message had been sent a few hours ago, while Jim had been out weeding. It read:

TY Phil, once again u r a STAR!!! I'll b there soon 2 pick up the spare keys. Don't tell J I'm w8ing for him @ the bungalow. Don't want him 2 do another runner!!! xxx

Jim's hands were so sweaty his fingers were almost too moist to scroll to the top of the conversation. The first message in the conversation, from a week ago, confirmed his worst fears:

EXCERPT FROM *RUN TO GROUND*

Hi Phil, sorry 2 bother u with a txt, but u've been so gr8 and I've been out of my mind since Jim took off. He got rid of his phone and everything. I have so many bills 2 pay and I'm due in just over a month. u don't no wot it means to finally find him. thnx Fi xxx

Jim thought Sloman had been a bit off with him for the past week and now he knew why. Fiona had tracked him down, but how? How had she known he was at the cemetery? Had she guessed why he really came to work here? She'd be the only one who could.

There was another tremor and Jim turned to look back into the office. For the first time he saw the huge hole in the corner. It had been behind him when he entered, so he hadn't seen it. The small pile of soil poking up through the hole began to shake and grow, sending loose earth onto the blood soaked floorboards.

The cloying smell wafted out of the office and Jim knew he had to get to the bungalow. He wasn't certain what he dreaded more, finding Fiona alive or dead.

THE END?

Not if you want to dive into more of Crystal Lake Publishing's Tales from the Darkest Depths!

Check out our amazing website and online store
or download our latest catalog here.
https://geni.us/CLPCatalog

Looking for award-winning Dark Fiction?
Download our latest catalog.

Includes our anthologies, novels, novellas, collections,
poetry, non-fiction, and specialty projects.

WHERE STORIES COME ALIVE!

We always have great new projects and content on the website to dive into, as well as a newsletter, behind the scenes options, social media platforms, our own dark fiction shared-world series and our very own webstore. Our webstore even has categories specifically for KU books, non-fiction, anthologies, and of course more novels and novellas.

ABOUT THE AUTHOR

Multiple award-winning author, Jasper Bark is infectious—and there's no known cure. If you're reading this you're already contaminated. The symptoms will manifest any time soon. There's nothing you can do about it. There's no itching or unfortunate rashes, but you'll become obsessed with his mind-bending books.

Then you'll want to tell everyone else about his visionary horror fiction. About its originality, its wild imagination and how it takes you to the edge of your sanity. We're afraid there's no way to avoid this. These words contain a power you're hopeless to resist. You're already in their thrall, you know you are. You're itching to read all of Jasper's bloodstained books. Don't fight this urge, embrace it. You've been bitten by the Bark bug and you love it!

Would you like to read five more of Jasper's books absolutely free?

Of course you would. I mean, who doesn't like free books?

Jasper's infamous novella, *Stuck On You* is now free to own as soon as you join Jasper's cult and sign up to his mailing list through the QR code below.

Don't worry, you won't have to shave your head or unalive any celebrities (for the first couple of years). But you will get all of Jasper's latest, videos, podcasts, blogs, breaking news on upcoming books and other crucial information to help you cyberstalk him.

What's more, you'll get two more short novels, a graphic novel and a spoof picture book, just to sweeten the deal! That's five free books just for signing up. These books are exclusive to this offer. You won't get them anywhere else.

Are we crazy? Of course we're crazy! We're asking you to join Jasper's cult!
And because we know you can't bear to miss out.

Don't be the only weird kid on your block to miss out. Don't delay. Sign up today.

Readers . . .

Thank you for reading *The Final Cut*. We hope you enjoyed this novel. If you have a moment, please review *The Final Cut* at the store where you bought it.

Help other readers by telling them why you enjoyed this book. No need to write an in-depth discussion. Even a single sentence will be greatly appreciated. Reviews go a long way to helping a book sell, and is great for an author's career. It'll also help us to continue publishing quality books.

Thank you again for taking the time to journey with Crystal Lake Publishing.

You will find links to all our social media platforms on our Linktree page.
https://linktr.ee/CrystalLakePublishing

MISSION STATEMENT

Since its founding in August 2012, Crystal Lake Publishing has quickly become one of the world's leading publishers of Dark Fiction and Horror books. In 2023, Crystal Lake Publishing formed a part of Crystal Lake Entertainment, joining several other divisions, including Torrid Waters, Crystal Lake Comics, Crystal Lake Kids, and many more.

While we strive to present only the highest quality fiction and entertainment, we also endeavour to support authors along their writing journey. We offer our time and experience in non-fiction projects, as well as author mentoring and services, at competitive prices.

With several Bram Stoker Award wins and many other wins and nominations (including the HWA's Specialty Press Award), Crystal Lake Publishing puts integrity, honor, and respect at the forefront of our publishing operations.

We strive for each book and outreach program we spearhead to not only entertain and touch or comment on issues that affect our readers, but also to strengthen and support the Dark Fiction field and its authors.

Not only do we find and publish authors we believe are destined for greatness, but we strive to work with men and women who endeavour to be decent human beings who care more for others than themselves, while still being hard working, driven, and passionate artists and storytellers.

Crystal Lake Publishing is and will always be a beacon of what passion and dedication, combined with overwhelming teamwork and respect, can accomplish. We endeavour to know each and every one of our readers, while building personal relationships with our authors, reviewers, bloggers, podcasters, bookstores, and libraries.

We will be as trustworthy, forthright, and transparent as any business can be, while also keeping most of the headaches away from our authors, since it's our job to solve the problems so they can stay in a creative mind. Which of course also means paying our authors.

We do not just publish books, we present to you worlds within your world, doors within your mind, from talented authors who sacrifice so much for a moment of your time.

There are some amazing small presses out there,

and through collaboration and open forums we will continue to support other presses in the goal of helping authors and showing the world what quality small presses are capable of accomplishing. No one wins when a small press goes down, so we will always be there to support hardworking, legitimate presses and their authors. We don't see Crystal Lake as the best press out there, but we will always strive to be the best, strive to be the most interactive and grateful, and even blessed press around. No matter what happens over time, we will also take our mission very seriously while appreciating where we are and enjoying the journey.

What do we offer our authors that they can't do for themselves through self-publishing?

We are big supporters of self-publishing (especially hybrid publishing), if done with care, patience, and planning. However, not every author has the time or inclination to do market research, advertise, and set up book launch strategies. Although a lot of authors are successful in doing it all, strong small presses will always be there for the authors who just want to do what they do best: write.

What we offer is experience, industry knowledge, contacts and trust built up over years. And due to our strong brand and trusting fanbase, every Crystal Lake Publishing book comes with weight of respect. In time our fans begin to trust our judgment and will try a new author purely based on our support of said author.

With each launch we strive to fine-tune our approach, learn from our mistakes, and increase our reach. We continue to assure our authors that we're here for them and that we'll carry the weight of the launch and dealing with third parties while they focus on their strengths—be it writing, interviews, blogs, signings, etc.

We also offer several mentoring packages to authors that include knowledge and skills they can use in both traditional and self-publishing endeavours.

We look forward to launching many new careers.

This is what we believe in. What we stand for. This will be our legacy.

Welcome to Crystal Lake Publishing— Tales from the Darkest Depths.

www.ingramcontent.com/pod-product-compliance
Lightning Source LLC
Chambersburg PA
CBHW071745190726
48292CB00003B/875